LAID BARE

ANNA STONE

© 2020 Anna Stone

All rights reserved. No part of this publication may be replicated, reproduced, or redistributed in any form without the prior written consent of the publisher.

This is a work of fiction. Names, characters, places, and incidents either are the products of the author's imagination or are used fictitiously. Any resemblance to actual persons, living or dead, businesses, companies, events, or locales is entirely coincidental.

ISBN: 9781922685018

CHAPTER 1

"Welcome to Mistress Media." The receptionist gave Blair a wide smile. "How can I help you?"

Blair cleared her throat. "I'm Blair Chase. I have an appointment with Madison Sloane."

"You're the journalism student?"

Blair nodded.

"One moment." The woman typed something into the computer behind the desk. "Madison is on a call right now, but she'll see you as soon as she's done. I'll take you through to her office."

Blair followed the woman through the bustling, open-plan office. It was huge, taking up the entire top floor of the sixty-story building. A sea of glass walls increased the illusion of space and allowed a view of the sprawling city below.

She looked around in awe. Working at a place like Mistress Media was her dream. She was in her final year of her journalism degree, just weeks from graduating. At twenty-five, it had been a long time coming. All Blair had to do was complete her final assignment—interviewing a person of her choice and writing an in-depth article about them.

Blair had chosen Madison Sloane, the CEO of Mistress Media. She'd emailed Madison several times without really expecting a response. Madison was a busy woman, after all. But in the end, Blair had gotten her attention.

They reached the back of the office. The receptionist gestured toward a door. "That's Madison's office. She knows you're here. Take a seat."

Blair thanked the woman and headed toward the door. Through the glass, a tall woman in a stylish but professional blue dress paced around in measured strides, a small Bluetooth headset in her ear. Her wavy brown hair was pulled back in a loose bun, and a touch of red lipstick graced her lips.

Madison Sloane, in the flesh. Journalist, CEO, billionaire, trailblazer, all before she'd turned thirty-five. The woman behind Mistress Media. The company had emerged a few years ago as an online publication with the mission of delivering everything from hard-hitting investigative pieces to articles on the latest fashions, all while being female-led. It was Madison Sloane's vision. She'd partnered with a handful of other women to further her goals, and within years, it had grown from a single publication to one of the biggest media empires in the world. And with it, Madison had become one of the wealthiest, most powerful women in the world.

But it wasn't Madison's wealth or power that Blair was interested in. It was the woman herself. Blair wanted to write an article on her that was personal rather than factual, to dig deep into the woman behind Mistress. Who was the real Madison Sloane? What fueled her?

But her interest in Madison wasn't just because of her assignment. The other, more personal, reasons for wanting to speak to her teased the back of Blair's mind.

Abruptly, Madison turned, her gaze locking onto Blair's through the glass. Blair's stomach fluttered. Madison's deep blue eyes were even more captivating in person than in all the photos of her in magazines.

She was so captivating.

After what seemed like an eternity, Madison swept her eyes up and down Blair's body, then she brought her hand up to her headset and turned and began pacing again.

Blair let out a breath and sat down. She needed to get into the right mindset for the interview. She'd prepared dozens of questions for Madison before narrowing them down to a smaller selection. There was so much Blair wanted to ask her. She'd read every single interview Madison had done, although they were few and far between, and she was determined not to waste time with the usual questions women like Madison were always asked. Madison had answered them all before, while politely rebuking the interviewers for not asking men the same questions. Questions about what it was like to be a female CEO. Questions about relationships. Questions relating to her sexuality.

The latter came up often in interviews with Madison. She'd always been open about being a lesbian. The fact that Madison was unashamed about her sexuality only fueled Blair's crush. Madison Sloane was everything Blair wanted to be.

Everything Blair wanted.

It didn't help that among the lady-loving ladies of the city, there were all kinds of rumors about Madison and the other women who led Mistress Media. The stories Blair had heard about Madison's romantic tastes would make anyone blush. Chances were, they were just stories. People liked to gossip.

But when Blair looked up at Madison again, she couldn't help but wonder if there was a thread of truth in those rumors. Everything about her spoke of a magnetic, commanding power. Was Madison like that behind closed doors too? Did she insist on taking control?

And why did Blair find the idea so alluring?

As if reading her mind, Madison looked up at Blair again. She still had her wireless earpiece in, her red lips moving in conversation, but her eyes remained fixed on Blair in a probing look that seemed to stretch on and on.

Heat rose up Blair's face. Madison's gaze did little to quell all the naughty thoughts in Blair's mind. She looked down at her notebook. When she glanced up again, Madison had her back to Blair.

She sighed. She needed to rein in her imagination.

Several minutes passed. Inside her office, Madison took a seat at her desk and started searching through files, still deep in conversation with whoever she was on the phone to. Blair looked at her watch. She'd been generously allocated forty-five minutes for the interview, but almost half that time had already passed.

Blair frowned. Had Madison forgotten about her? Or was she simply running late? Blair could wait. It was a Friday evening, and she had plans later in the night, but not for another hour or so. And it was nothing important. Blair had a date with a woman from a dating app who she'd never met. She wasn't exactly looking forward to it, but she'd been single for so long that she'd figured she should make an effort to go out and meet people.

Plus, she was going through a really long dry spell. She had an itch that needed to be scratched.

But Blair wasn't going to pass up this opportunity. Being here, seeing Madison Sloane in person, made Blair want to speak to her, to grab her attention even more.

Through the glass, Madison gave Blair another oblique glance, then turned to her laptop and began to type, still speaking into her headset.

Blair stretched out in her chair. She'd better get comfortable. She was going to get that interview with Madison, no matter what.

∽

Madison pulled the wireless earpiece out of her ear and began packing up her desk. As she did, her gaze returned to the chairs just outside her office. A woman sat in one of them, her sleek red hair gathered over one shoulder. She was dressed in a blouse, skirt, and sensible flats. The woman stared down at her notebook, chewing her lip with a look of intense concentration on her face.

Madison frowned. The red-haired woman had been sitting there for the last hour. Now and then, Madison had caught the woman staring. It was equal parts disconcerting and intriguing. What on earth did she want?

Madison didn't know what she was doing there, and

frankly, she'd been too busy to find out. She'd had three urgent phone calls in a row, with barely a moment to breathe in between, and she'd spent the last two calls answering emails while trying to sort out plans for a late business dinner. She and her COO were meeting with a pair of investors from Taiwan. She only had half an hour until she was due at the restaurant.

Madison picked up her briefcase and headed to the door. As soon as she opened it, the woman in the chair stood up. She was the same height as Madison but had a slighter frame. Up close, Madison could see that the woman's light skin had a slight flush, and she had a sprinkling of freckles on her nose and cheeks. Her eyes were an enticing mix of a dozen shades of brown. Something about those eyes triggered Madison's memory. But Madison didn't know her. She wouldn't have forgotten someone so striking.

"Ms. Sloane," the redhead said.

"Madison is fine." Tearing her eyes away from the woman, Madison started toward the front of the office, beckoning the woman to follow her. "What do you need?"

"I'm here to interview you."

Madison held back a curse. She'd completely forgotten. "You're the journalism student."

"Yes. I'm Blair."

That explained why she'd been staring at Madison the entire time. The receptionist had sent a message when Blair had arrived, but she'd promptly forgotten about it when another phone call had come through. It was unlike her to be so forgetful. Clearly, she was overworked.

"I apologize for keeping you waiting," Madison said.

"That's okay," Blair replied. "Thanks for agreeing to the interview."

"Yes, about that. I have somewhere to be tonight. I'll have my assistant call you to reschedule. I should have an opening in a month's time."

Blair stopped. "A month?" She sped up to catch up with Madison again. "But that's too late!"

"It's the best I can do."

"You don't understand. This is for a college assignment. The deadline is in two weeks."

"I'm sorry, but you'll have to find someone else to interview."

As Madison passed the reception desk, the receptionist called her name.

"Your assistant left this for you." She handed Madison a bottle of wine with a bow around the neck. "She said she couldn't find the '61 vintage, so she got the '64 instead."

"Thank you." The wine would make a fine gift for the investors Madison was meeting for dinner. "I'm done for the evening. I'll see you on Monday."

Madison turned to head toward the elevators, but Blair stepped in her path. Madison stared in surprise.

Blair met her gaze, unflinching. "What about the interview?"

Madison narrowed her eyes. "I told you, either wait a month or find someone else to interview."

Blair's expression set, the red tinge on her cheeks deepening. "You don't understand. I did hours of research and preparation for this. I don't want to interview anyone else."

"I don't have time for this." Madison stepped around the woman and headed to the bank of elevators. The light above one of them flicked on. Madison didn't want to miss it. The trip from the top floor to the ground took forever, and she didn't want to have to wait for another elevator.

"I waited two hours to see you," Blair said from behind her. "It has to be you, Madison."

Madison stopped, her irritation growing. She turned and regarded Blair. Once again, Madison was gripped with the sensation that she knew the woman somehow, but she pushed it aside.

"I was doing you a favor by agreeing to this interview," Madison said crisply. "But it isn't going to happen tonight. Making a scene in my office isn't going to change that. It's going to make me even less inclined to work with you on this."

"I'm sorry," Blair said quickly. "Just give me half an hour. Fifteen minutes, even." Her lips curved in a cajoling smile that didn't soften the intensity in her eyes.

Madison examined her. If Blair hadn't been hounding her moments ago, Madison would have admired her fierce determination. No, more than that—she would have found it appealing. She liked a woman who knew what she wanted. And she liked to make those kinds of women unravel even more.

It was interesting how many strong, determined women wanted just that.

Madison remembered something. "You're the student who sent me all those emails."

Blair nodded. "I had to get your attention somehow."

Those emails were why Madison had agreed to the interview in the first place. Blair had made it impossible to ignore her. That had been weeks ago. She'd forgotten about them until now.

Madison looked her up and down. It was clear that she wasn't giving up. Madison suspected that anyone this tenacious was going to ask her all kinds of questions, which was the last thing she needed. She didn't like people digging around in her life.

So why did Madison feel the inexplicable desire to give the woman a moment of her time?

"Remind me," Madison said. "What's your last name"

"It's Chase. Blair Chase." She held out a slender hand.

Madison took it slowly, intrigued by the gentle pressure Blair exerted and the tingle it sent up Madison's arm. She withdrew. "Well, Blair, if you're set on interviewing me, you'll have to do it on the go. I'm heading to dinner across town. The drive will take twenty minutes. Ride with me. You can ask me all the questions you like."

"Really?" Blair's face lit up, then returned to a neutral expression, as if she was trying to maintain a professional demeanor. "Yes. Okay."

The elevator dinged, and the doors opened. It was empty. Madison and Blair stepped inside. Madison pushed the button for the ground floor and suppressed the tiny flurry of panic she always felt when stepping into elevators. She did this several times a day. She'd had to learn to deal with her fears when she'd bought an office at the top of a skyscraper years ago.

Or perhaps that was why she'd chosen this office in the first place.

The doors closed, and the elevator descended.

"Why don't we get started now?" Madison said. "I'm assuming you have questions prepared?"

"Yes, they're right here." Blair opened her notebook.

The lights in the elevator flickered. A loud clunk came from somewhere above them.

Blair looked up. "Wha—"

The lights went out. A loud screeching filled the air. The elevator dropped, fast. Madison grabbed onto the handrail behind her, her stomach turning to ice.

The elevator lurched to a stop.

The screeching was replaced by silence.

The darkness remained.

CHAPTER 2

Dread consumed Madison's body. Although the elevator had stopped falling, it wasn't moving. She was trapped in a tiny box, in the dark, high above the ground with no air, something heavy and solid pushing against her chest. So hard against her that she couldn't breathe—

The lights flickered back on. She looked down. Blair was pressed against her, one arm clutching Madison's shoulder, the other on the wall next to her, holding herself up.

Madison took a deep breath. She'd forgotten all about Blair. And while Madison had been holding onto the handrail when the elevator had gone into free-fall, Blair had been holding her notebook. It was on the floor now, along with the bottle of wine Madison had been holding, which was thankfully still intact. If she hadn't grabbed onto Madison, Blair would probably be on the floor too.

Blair looked back at Madison, her face turning crimson. "Sorry!" She jerked back. "I lost my balance."

"It's fine." Madison swallowed. With the lights back on,

the space inside the elevator seemed less oppressive. But it was still small. And they were still trapped.

She glanced around. *Think, Madison.* They had to get out of the elevator. Her eyes landed on the elevator panel. Beneath the buttons for each floor was a large red button with a phone symbol on it.

Of course. Madison stepped toward the panel and pressed the emergency call button. She waited, but no sound came from the speaker. She pressed again; once, twice, three times.

Nothing.

Panic welling up inside her, Madison jabbed the button to open the door. There was a chance that the elevator had stopped at a floor and they could just walk right out.

The door didn't budge.

Cursing, Madison yanked her phone out of her briefcase. As expected, she had no cell signal. Even the building's Wi-Fi didn't penetrate the elevator shaft.

She turned to Blair. "Your cell phone. Do you have a signal?"

Blair grabbed her phone from her bag on the floor. "Nope. Nothing."

Madison hammered the emergency call button over and over. It couldn't possibly be broken. If it was, it meant they were trapped. No one knew where they were. How long would it take for security to realize there was a problem? Minutes? Hours? Days, even? There were other elevators in the building. No one would notice if one wasn't moving. And it was nighttime now, on a Friday. Almost everyone had gone home. No one would be back until tomorrow.

They'd be trapped all night.

Madison's heart thudded rapidly against her chest. She couldn't possibly be trapped inside this tiny, windowless box. Not again. Her chest tightened. The lights were still on, but darkness encroached on the corners of her vision. The walls began to shrink even further as thick, cold tendrils of fear gripped her—

"Madison?"

She felt a hand on her shoulder and looked up. Blair was next to her, staring back at her with concern.

Madison looked down at Blair's hand.

"I'm sorry!" Blair pulled away. "You weren't answering me. You looked all spaced out."

"It's fine." Madison had been distantly aware of Blair saying her name, but she'd been paralyzed by fear.

"Are you all right?"

"Yes." Madison took a few calming breaths. It did nothing to slow her pounding heart. "I don't like enclosed spaces, that's all."

Blair frowned. "You're claustrophobic?"

"Mildly." Madison had thought she'd gotten over it a long time ago. Apparently not.

"Are you going to be okay?"

"Yes." *I'm fine. I can handle this.*

"I'm sure someone knows the elevator is stuck. Maintenance or whoever. They're probably fixing it as we speak."

"You're right." In a building this modern, there had to be safeguards. But Madison's current anxiety had nothing to do with logic.

"Is there anything I can do to help?" Blair asked.

"No," Madison snapped. "I'm fine."

Blair took a step back. "Okay."

Madison felt a twinge of guilt. "I'm sorry. This is a stressful situation for me." She wasn't used to being vulnerable. And she didn't like it.

"That's okay. I understand. If there's anything I can do, let me know."

Madison closed her eyes and took a few more deep breaths. There was something in Blair's voice, her presence, that had a soothing effect. Slowly, her pulse began to return to a normal speed, and her head began to clear.

She opened her eyes. Blair was still looking at her with worried eyes, as if she were afraid Madison was going to descend into panic at any moment. Madison certainly felt that way. If she was going to get through this, she needed something to take her mind off things.

Perhaps Blair could be that something.

"Actually," Madison said. "There is something you can do to help."

"Sure. Anything."

Madison's lip curled in a small smile. Blair certainly was eager. "I could use a distraction. Just until we get out of here."

"Okay." Blair paused in thought. "We could play a game."

"A game?"

"Like twenty questions."

Madison sighed. This wasn't going to work.

"Let me think of something else." Blair looked around. "I know. How about I interview you?"

Madison scoffed. "You want to interview me? Right now?"

"Why not?" Blair gave her an innocent shrug. "You want a distraction. It'll help pass the time."

Madison studied her. She still couldn't shake the feeling she knew Blair somehow. And why was Blair so intent on interviewing her? Was there more behind the way Blair looked at her than just professional interest? Madison couldn't deny she felt drawn to Blair, in more ways than one. She had this fieriness about her that Madison found so appealing.

Madison steadied herself. She shouldn't have been thinking about a woman she'd just met that way, and not when they were stuck in close quarters together. Clearly, the stress of the situation was getting to her.

"All right," Madison said. "Let's get started."

~

Blair picked up her notebook from the floor. "Let me find my notes." She flipped through it, stalling, buying time to collect herself. The elevator breaking down wasn't all that had her flustered. The fact that she'd ended up falling onto Madison, her hand dangerously close to Madison's chest, had her mortified. A few inches lower, and things would have been far more awkward.

But Madison had barely noticed in her rattled state. Blair was surprised by Madison's reaction to the situation. Blair knew phobias weren't rational, but she hadn't expected to see Madison Sloane so shaken.

Blair glanced at her. She seemed far calmer than she had been moments ago, but the hint of tension in her body suggested that she was trying hard to hold herself together. Blair herself was doing the same thing. She didn't mind being stuck in an enclosed space, but she wasn't thrilled about the fact that they were suspended hundreds of feet above the ground in a broken-down elevator. She couldn't help but wonder if they would plunge to their deaths at any second, as she'd been so certain was going to happen just moments ago. They were probably safe. The brakes had kicked in quickly. It was more likely they'd simply be stuck until someone realized the elevator had malfunctioned.

"Well?" Madison said. "You were practically begging me for an interview before we got into this mess."

A shiver rolled down Blair's neck. Madison's firm but honeyed voice was hypnotic. Blair got the feeling that Madison could have told her to do anything with that voice, and she'd be powerless to refuse.

Get a grip, Blair. She was stuck in an elevator with Madison for God knew how long. She had to keep her head.

"I'm ready," Blair said. "Mind if I record this?"

"Go ahead," Madison said.

Blair tucked her notebook under her arm and started the recording app on her phone. It would probably have been smarter to try to save her battery just in case, but this was important. "I was thinking we could start with a few questions about Mistress Media, then move on to some more personal subjects."

Madison frowned. "Personal subjects?"

"Well, yeah. My assignment is to write a detailed, personal portrait of my subject. I mentioned it in my emails."

Madison sighed. "All right. Go on then."

Blair flipped to the page in her notebook where her questions for Madison began. "So, why did you start Mistress Media?"

Madison raised an eyebrow. "If you want to work for anything other than small-town newspapers, you're going to have to come up with more engaging questions."

Madison's scolding tone made Blair's skin heat up. "This is just the warm-up."

"If you say so." Madison leaned back against the handrail. "I started Mistress Media because of the lack of female representation in the journalism landscape. Mistress was my way of rectifying that."

"Is that why Mistress is female run?"

"Partially. While we consider everyone equally for leadership positions, we make sure women are given representation they deserve. The executive team is all female because when I started the company, I recruited from among my friends, most of whom are women."

Madison's executive team consisted of herself and several other women, all rich, brilliant, and gorgeous, who helmed Mistress Media together.

"You all went to Moore University, right?" Blair asked.

"We did, but we were in different cohorts. You're studying at Moore too, aren't you?"

Blair stumbled over her words. "Yes. How do you know?"

"You mentioned it in one of your emails."

Right. That made perfect sense. For a moment, Blair had thought that Madison actually remembered her.

Collecting herself, Blair moved onto the next question. "Why did you choose the name 'Mistress Media?'"

A slight smile crossed Madison's lips. "You like the name, do you?"

"It's interesting, that's all."

"Our original online publication was called *Mistress*, so when we began to expand, we took it on as the company name. The idea behind the Mistress name is simple. The definition of the word is 'a woman in a position of power, authority or control.' The name reflects the fact that Mistress Media is all about empowering women, both our employees and our readers, through journalism and social change."

"And that's all there is to it?"

"Why do you ask?"

"It's just that, the word 'mistress' has other connotations."

Blair was going off script, but she was suddenly curious. The word *mistress* conjured up an image in her mind that went beyond 'a woman in control.' And with all those rumors she'd heard about Madison Sloane, she couldn't help but wonder if there was more to the name.

"You're right," Madison said. "Mistress is a subversive word. And there's power in that. It's bold and unflinching, just like the women who run Mistress and who read it. But all those undertones are secondary. Whatever meaning anyone chooses to assign to our name is up to them." Madison folded her arms over her chest, her gaze piercing. "Perhaps the meaning you've chosen says something about you."

Warmth rose up Blair's cheeks. "I'm just curious, that's all."

"Curiosity is good, but if you're not careful, you could find yourself in trouble." Madison lowered her voice. "But something tells me you're the type that doesn't mind getting into a little trouble."

What was Blair supposed to say to that? Madison was still looking at her, those blue eyes of hers like super-hot flames.

"There's something I'm curious about," Madison said. "Why did you want to interview me so badly?"

Blair averted her gaze. "Like I said, I need to do this assignment. It's due in two weeks."

"That's not what I meant. Why me specifically? You could have chosen anyone, but it's clear you were set on interviewing me. You sent so many emails. Most people would have given up sooner."

"Right," Blair said sheepishly. Perhaps she'd gone overboard. "Sorry about that."

"It's fine. Why do you think I agreed to the interview?" Madison leaned toward her. "I like a determined woman. And your emails intrigued me."

"You actually read them?"

"Of course. I make it a point to read all my emails, although I don't always reply to them personally. I was planning to have my assistant draft a polite response turning you down. But when the emails just kept coming, it made me want to know why you were so persistent."

"I... I just thought you'd make a good interview subject. You're one of the most successful women in the world. You have an interesting story. And you seem like my kind of woman." Christ, what was she saying? Telling Madison the truth would have been less awkward than this.

Madison's lips curled up at the corners, her gaze knowing. "Your kind of woman?"

"In the sense that I respect you. That's all I meant."

"I don't think it was what you meant."

Suddenly, Blair noticed that the elevator was getting warm. Had the air conditioning broken too? The lights were still on, so the electricity was still working at least. Perhaps it was just their body heat.

Not that Madison's body was hot.

Blair took a deep breath, gathering herself. "I admire you as a journalist and a businesswoman. You're a great writer. You've built this media empire and have become this bastion of female empowerment. I want to have a career like yours."

"So, what is it?"

"That's it."

Madison said nothing. Blair wasn't sure if Madison believed her, but at least she'd dropped the subject. "Let's move on." Blair looked down at her notes. "Since starting Mistress several years ago, it has grown from a single publication to an international media empire. What do you credit your success to?"

"I can't take all the credit," Madison said. "Everything I've built was only possible due to the hard work of not only myself, but the other women who I run Mistress with."

Blair asked Madison a few more questions about Mistress Media and the team that ran it. Madison answered them all with poise. There was no sign that just minutes ago, she'd appeared to be on the verge of panic.

It almost made Blair feel bad about all the probing questions she was planning to spring on her. Madison Sloane was notoriously private when it came to anything beyond the superficial details of her life. But Blair was determined to dig deeper.

She shut her notebook. She had all the important questions filed away in her mind. "Let's move on to some questions about you."

"Ah, yes," Madison said. "I'm sure you'll want to hear about all about my childhood? My family?"

"I already know everything I need to know. I've read all your other interviews." Blair knew Madison had grown up right here in the city to a wealthy family. She knew Madison had studied journalism and business at Moore. She even knew the names of Madison's parents and sisters. That wasn't what Blair meant by 'personal.'

"What made you decide to start Mistress?" Blair asked.

"You already asked me that." There was a hint of irritation in Madison's voice.

"I asked you why you started Mistress. What I want to know is, what was it that inspired you to do so?"

"It's simple. Mistress was born from a desire to do something meaningful with my life. I'm lucky enough to come from a privileged background. So, I decided it was important to do something with all the gifts I'd been given."

It was a stock answer, delivered in a practiced manner. But Blair didn't want that. She wanted something real. She looked at Madison. What was going on underneath the depths of those cool blue eyes?

"Was there something that triggered this realization?" Blair asked.

"Nothing specific. Just life experience."

"There's a period in your late twenties where there's a gap in your life after you quit your job at The New York Press. You disappeared for two years."

"I decided to take some time off to travel." Madison

uncrossed her arms, tucked a stray strand of hair behind her ear, then crossed them again. "That's all."

"Did your travels help you figure out what you wanted to do with your life?"

Madison scoffed softly. "My travels were a misguided youthful attempt to find myself, nothing more."

"Did it work? Did you find yourself? The timeline fits. It was right before you started Mistress."

Madison narrowed her eyes. "How do you know so much about what I did in my twenties?"

"Research. Articles, interviews, social media, the newspaper you used to work for." *Great, now I sound like a stalker.* "It was all for the assignment. It's easy to find information on people these days."

"Well, there's no story there. All I got from my travels was a bad case of the stomach flu."

"Then what was your inspiration? What—"

"A word of advice," Madison interjected. "From one journalist to another. Don't treat interviews like interrogations. Be diplomatic. If your subject is reluctant to talk about something, don't push them, or they'll clam up. You won't get a second chance."

It was then that Blair noticed Madison's discomfort. Her entire body was stiff, and her eyes were cold, her face marked with tension. Blair had gotten carried away.

"Sorry. Let's move on to something else."

Madison raised her palm. "No. We're done."

CHAPTER 3

Madison kicked off her heels, removed her coat and folded it neatly on top of her briefcase in the corner. It was getting warm. How long had they been in this damn elevator? Madison was trying her hardest not to think about it.

She looked at Blair out of the corner of her eye. Madison's words to her had come out harsher than she'd intended, but Blair had been getting dangerously close to a subject Madison didn't want to talk about.

Madison got the sense that she wasn't the only one keeping things close to the chest. When she'd questioned Blair about why she really wanted to interview Madison, Blair had gotten flustered. Or perhaps that was simply because Madison hadn't been able to resist pushing Blair's buttons slightly.

Madison looked Blair up and down. She couldn't deny that she was developing an interest in Blair that was entirely unprofessional…

She pushed her thoughts aside. What was important right now was simply getting along with Blair.

Madison turned to her. "Blair, I apologize for being short with you just now."

"It's fine. I shouldn't have pried."

Silence stretched between them. Beside her, Blair dug into her bag and pulled out a bottle of water.

She took a long swig before holding it out to Madison. "Want some?"

Madison shook her head. "I have a bottle of water in my briefcase. And it's not a good idea to drink too much. You know, in case we're stuck in here for a while."

"Oh. I didn't even think about that." Alarm crossed Blair's face. "We're not going to be stuck in here for that long, are we? Surely someone knows we're in here by now, right?"

Madison felt a wave of nausea. "Yes. I'm sure they do."

"Crap. I didn't mean to make you nervous."

"No, you're right. It has been a long time now." Madison checked her watch. It was half-past ten. She didn't remember exactly when they'd gotten into the elevator, but it had been at least an hour ago. "We should start thinking about what happens if we don't get out of here soon." Her pulse sped up again.

"Well, we both have water. I think I have a granola bar in my purse." Blair rummaged around in her bag and pulled something out. "Here. Two granola bars. And a chocolate bar."

"All I have is this bottle of wine. It's not going to be any use to us unless we run out of water and get desperate."

"We're definitely not going to be in here for that long."

Blair put her purse back down. "Do you want to sit down? There isn't much room, but it's better than standing up."

"Good idea."

Madison spread her coat on the floor. Blair placed hers next to Madison's. They sat on the floor, their backs against the wall. There was enough room to stretch out their legs if they sat side-by-side, but that was all. The elevator was relatively spacious, but they wouldn't be able to stretch out fully if they wanted to.

They wouldn't need to sleep in here, would they? A sudden dizziness overcame her. She tipped her head back against the wall, her breath growing shallower. With each minute that passed, it seemed more and more likely that no one knew they were in here at all.

"Madison?" Blair said. "Are you okay?"

Madison swallowed the lump in her throat. "Yes." A lie.

She drew in a long, slow breath, then another, trying to think back to all those techniques her therapist had taught her. But her mind had gone blank. The familiar fear threatening to overtake her was too strong. She couldn't bear the thought of spending the night in this tiny, windowless room, with no sign of rescue. She couldn't go through that again.

An invisible hand squeezed inside Madison's chest. She couldn't breathe. Were they running out of air? That was impossible. But no matter how hard Madison breathed, her lungs struggled to get enough oxygen, as if they were paralyzed. It was as if her whole body was paralyzed, an inescapable weight crushing down on her—

"Madison," Blair said. "Talk to me. Tell me what's going on."

Madison blinked. "I—" Her mouth was dry. "I'm having a panic attack." She hadn't had one in a long time, but she knew what they felt like. The fact that she knew she was having a panic attack didn't change how she was feeling.

"Oh." Blair paused. "Does this happen often?"

"No," Madison said between breaths. "But it's not often that I'm stuck in a damned elevator."

"Just try to remember, you're perfectly safe."

"The hell I am." Madison's voice cracked. "We're trapped in here."

Blair maintained her composure. "Yes, but it's only temporary. We're going to get out of here. Someone is going to come for us."

And if no one came? A cold numbness crept up her arms and legs. They were going to die in here.

"Madison," Blair said, "Look at me."

Madison lifted her head. Blair stared at her intensely, her hand on Madison's upper arm.

"Just breathe. No, not like that. Slowly."

That was simple. Madison could do that. She slowed her breaths, fighting the air-starved feeling gripping her whole body.

"I'm right here, Madison. Stay with me. Keep breathing."

Blair took Madison's hand. It felt warm and soft, enough to pull Madison back to reality. But Madison was still on the edge of panic, threatening to teeter back over it at any moment. In normal circumstances, she would have been able to fend her anxiety off by escaping the situation that was causing it, but she was trapped in here, and would be for God knew how long—

"Madison. Everything is going to be okay."

Madison echoed Blair's words. "Everything is going to be okay."

Blair continued to speak, her voice a low, soothing drone. Madison focused on the words, each one a brick in the wall of calm she was building. Her heart slowed down. The clenching in her chest relaxed. But her body was still abuzz with adrenaline. She looked down at her hand. Blair hadn't let go, and despite Madison's state, Blair's touch stirred something inside her.

"See, you're okay," Blair said. "We're okay. We're going to get out of here in no time. All we have to do is pass the time until then. Why don't we just talk while we wait?"

Madison took a few deep breaths. "All right."

"Let's get to know each other. Completely off the record, I promise."

Madison nodded. She certainly didn't want to answer more of Blair's interview questions, but simply talking with her would be a welcome distraction. And no small part of her wanted to get to know Blair. "What do you want to talk about?"

"I haven't thought that far ahead yet," Blair said sheepishly. "How about this? What's your favorite food?"

A simple question. Madison could handle that. "Mushroom Florentine."

"That makes my answer sound childish. It's carrot cake. What can I say, I like simple pleasures." Blair drew her fingers through her hair, deep in thought. "Cats or dogs?"

"You really go for the hard-hitting questions, don't you?" The hammering in Madison's chest had reduced to a light flutter now.

Blair crossed her arms in mock offense. "I'd like to see you do better. Personally, I'm a dog person."

"Cats," Madison said. "Dogs need too much attention."

"That's why I like them better. They're always so appreciative of whatever love you give them. Why don't you ask me something?"

Madison thought for a moment. "What's your favorite sport?"

Blair paused. "Basketball, maybe? I don't really follow sports. What about you?"

"Ice hockey. It's not that I get excited about watching men barge into each other with sticks. My mother is Canadian. When we were kids, we'd visit her parents in Edmonton and they'd take us to hockey games. I always liked the atmosphere."

"Huh. I didn't know that about you."

"Not everything about someone can be found online. Research can only take you so far. It's your turn."

Blair was quiet for a moment. "Is there anyone special in your life? You know, like, a girlfriend or a partner?"

Madison let out a soft chuckle. "I take back what I said. You do know how to ask hard-hitting questions."

Blair gave her an innocent shrug. "We're supposed to be getting to know each other."

"If you did all this research about me, you should know the answer."

"I do. I just wanted to hear it from you."

"The answer is no. I'm very much single." Madison stretched her legs out in front of her. "Finding someone who is compatible with my lifestyle is difficult."

"Your lifestyle?"

"You know. Fast-paced, high-pressure, long work hours. Making time for a partner can be difficult. I need someone who understands that." Madison turned to Blair. "Besides, I have very specific tastes which most women don't share. In fact, some people find those tastes off-putting."

Blair bit her lip. "What kind of tastes?"

Madison gave her a hard look. "You've had your chance. It's my turn to ask a question now."

A pink flush crept up Blair's cheeks. It wasn't the first time a firm comment or the slightest hint of suggestion from Madison had elicited that reaction from her.

Madison asked Blair another question, something completely innocent. As Blair replied, Madison's eyes wandered down to her lips. They were full and soft, and almost hypnotic.

As they continued to chat, Madison's anxiety faded into the background. Madison was usually a private person, but for some reason, Blair was easy to open up to, her sweet smile disarming.

"What are you smiling about?" Madison asked.

Blair shrugged. "Nothing. I was just thinking, of all the people to be stuck in an elevator with, being in here with you isn't so bad. Not that I want to be trapped in here, obviously. Or for you to be trapped with me. I—"

Madison held up her hand. "It's fine, I understand. And you're certainly one of the more interesting women I've spent a Friday night with." She fixed her gaze on Blair. "Although those nights usually end very differently to how I suspect ours is going to."

Blair took a strand of her hair, curling it around her

finger in the most tantalizing way. "And how do those nights usually end?"

"A lady doesn't kiss and tell. But I'm sure you can use your imagination."

Blair's lips parted slightly, the look on her face telling Madison that she was doing exactly what Madison had suggested. Madison couldn't deny her own internal thrill.

What the hell was she doing, flirting so shamelessly with this stranger she was trapped with? At least, Madison's behavior was shameless by her standards. She was normally far more restrained. Clearly, being stuck in this box was making her lose her inhibitions.

No, that was a lie. She couldn't truly blame what she felt toward Blair on the situation. If they'd met in another time and place, Madison wouldn't have thought twice about asking Blair out for a drink, or two, or three, which would inevitably lead to far more.

What would it be like to draw her fingers through Blair's vibrant, silken hair, to take her by the waist and pull her in close, to wipe that smile off her face with a kiss? What kind of woman would Blair be when the lights went out? Would she retain that same headstrong demeanor? Or would she beg Madison to put her in her place?

Madison snuck another glance at Blair. It was that exact combination of strength and tenacity along with a desire to have someone else lead behind closed doors that Madison found so intoxicating. Was it a combination that Blair possessed?

Did Madison dare try to find out?

CHAPTER 4

Blair looked at the time on her phone. It was almost midnight. They'd been in the elevator for hours.

Madison peered at Blair's screen. "Looks like I missed my dinner meeting." She looked up at Blair. "Did you have plans tonight? It's a Friday, after all."

"I did, but I canceled them while I was waiting for you."

Madison grimaced. "Sorry for keeping you. Was it anything important?"

"Just a date. Well, not an actual date." Blair didn't want Madison to get the wrong impression, although it was ridiculous to think that Madison Sloane cared about Blair's love life in the first place. "It was with a woman I've been talking to on some dating app. It's just been a while since I've had a girlfriend, so I thought I'd make an effort in that department. Not that I was expecting any romance tonight, but I'm going through a bit of a dry spell…" Heat crept up Blair's face. "You probably didn't need to know that."

"Blair, we've been stuck in a four-foot box together for several hours. As far as I'm concerned, there's no such thing as oversharing. Nothing is off-limits. You can tell me anything you want."

Blair chewed her lip. Was now a good time to come clean about why she'd been so determined to interview Madison in the first place?

Madison leaned toward Blair. "What happens in this elevator stays in this elevator."

Suddenly Blair's thoughts of confessing were forgotten. What exactly was Madison expecting to happen?

"You know what?" Madison said. "I want to make it up to you for making you miss your date."

"It's not a big deal," Blair said. "Really."

"No, I insist. And it isn't like we have anything else to do."

Blair hesitated. "What did you have in mind? There isn't much we can do while we're stuck in here."

"We are. But we have food. And we have wine. It was supposed to be a gift for the investors I was meeting for dinner tonight, but since that's not happening, why don't we have a taste? It's an excellent vintage."

Blair gave her a side-long look. "Are you sure that's a good idea? Should we really be drinking right now?"

"A few mouthfuls can't hurt." Madison reached over and picked up the bottle. "Why don't we open it up, along with the granola bars and chocolate and have a little date of our own?"

Blair's heart skipped a beat. Had Madison just asked her on a date? No one in their right mind would ask someone on a date under such unusual circumstances. Even at the best of times, there was no way a woman like Madison Sloane would ask Blair on a date.

And yet, Madison had been making suggestive remarks the entire time they'd been talking. And every time she did, Blair felt herself blush like a schoolgirl. There was something about Madison that had her mesmerized. It went far beyond the admiration she'd always held toward the woman as a journalist. It even went beyond how deeply attractive Blair found her. Because there was no doubt about that. Madison was stunning. And even after being trapped in this hot, stuffy elevator for hours on end, Madison still looked elegant and flawless.

She still had that same presence that demanded Blair's attention.

"Well?" Madison brandished the bottle of wine. "What do you say?"

"Sure," Blair replied. "It's a date."

Madison set the bottle down and opened her briefcase. "Let's see if I have something in here to get the cork out."

"I'll get the food." Blair pulled out the granola bars and chocolate out of her purse, setting them on her coat between herself and Madison as if it were a picnic blanket. Compared to the wine, which bore an old, expensive-looking label, it wasn't much. At least the chocolate was the fancy almond kind Blair liked.

"This will work." Madison took her keys from the front pocket of her briefcase and stabbed it into the cork of the wine bottle, prizing it out with a pop. The heady aroma of red wine filled the air, adding to the stuffy atmosphere in the elevator. Madison didn't seem to mind. Her panic was long gone. So was Blair's.

Her heart was racing for entirely different reasons now.

"No glasses, I'm afraid. We'll have to pass the bottle." Madison held it out toward Blair. "You first."

Blair took a sip. "Wow. This tastes incredible." She didn't know anything about wine, but she knew this was good. She'd never had anything like it.

Blair handed the bottle back to Madison before she could drink too much. There were lots of practical reasons why getting drunk while stuck in an elevator was a bad idea. But mostly, she didn't want to lose her head around Madison. She'd already put her foot in it several times. Who knew what would happen with alcohol thrown into the mix?

She might just say all those indecent thoughts she was having about Madison out loud.

Madison took a drink, her red lips pursing around the mouth of the bottle. She set it down between them. A tinge of red wine was left on her lips. And what perfect lips they were.

Blair's stomach rumbled audibly. She hadn't eaten since before she arrived at Madison's office. She handed Madison a granola bar, before taking the other one for herself.

"A main course of granola bars, followed by chocolate for dessert." Madison unwrapped her granola bar and took a bite, chewing and swallowing with effort. "It isn't exactly fine dining, but we'll have to make do."

"To be honest, this is probably better than the date I was supposed to go on," Blair said. "It was at this dodgy-looking dive bar. She picked the venue, not me."

Madison tilted her head, examining Blair. "Do you often let the other woman take the lead in a relationship? You don't strike me as the type."

"That depends on what part of the relationship we're talking about."

"What part do you think we're talking about?"

Blair lowered her gaze slightly. "The fun part."

A barely perceptible smirk crossed Madison's lips. "I thought that might be the case. I've always liked that in a woman. Strength in all things that matter, an enthusiastic vulnerability when it comes to intimacy."

She held the bottle of wine out to Blair. Blair grabbed it, their fingertips touching, desire crackling up her hand and arm like electricity.

Madison didn't let go of the bottle. Her eyes locked on to Blair's. "There's nothing more irresistible than a woman who knows what she wants."

Blair's breath caught. Madison released the bottle and sat back, watching her. As Blair drank the smooth, sweet wine down, she was keenly aware that just moments ago, Madison's lips had been where her own were now. The faint taste of Madison's lipstick rimmed the bottle.

What would Madison's lips taste like?

Blair's whole body flushed. She set the wine down and unwrapped the bar of chocolate before offering it to Madison.

Madison broke off a square. "The woman you were supposed to go on a date with tonight wasn't worth your while. A dive bar? I'd never take a woman somewhere like that."

Blair tried her hardest to hold her question back, but she couldn't resist. "If you were to take a woman on a date, where would you take her?"

"*Where* I'd take her isn't what's important. It's about how I'd treat her."

Madison broke off another piece of chocolate and slipped it between her lips.

"First, I'd take her to dinner. Somewhere nice, so she could experience the finest of culinary delights. An appetizer for the pleasures to come."

The way the word 'pleasures' rolled off Madison's tongue sent a flicker of heat through Blair's core.

"After dinner, we'd have drinks," Madison continued. "Somewhere small and quiet where we could spend hours undisturbed. I'd take that time to get to know her intimately, to get her all worked up about what the rest of the night will hold."

Blair could imagine it already. Her, with Madison, sitting side-by-side, talking the night away. They were already sitting close. It was unavoidable in the space they were in. While at first it had felt stifling, now it was electrifying.

"And just when she'd start to feel like she couldn't take it any longer, I'd invite her back to my apartment. To my bedroom." Madison's silky voice dropped an octave, smoothed into a subtle croon. "And I'd spend the entire night torturing her with pleasure so intense that she'd feel like she was the only woman in the world."

Blair let out a light breath, an unmistakable throbbing within her. "That's... an interesting choice of words."

A smile grew on Madison's ruby red lips. "What do you mean?"

"Torture. You said you'd 'torture' her with pleasure."

"Did I? I was speaking figuratively. Any woman I'd take

into my bed would be one hundred percent willing. She'd be more than willing. More than eager. She'd be begging for the sweet agony that only I could provide her with." Madison leaned closer. "I like a woman who knows what she wants. And I like it even more when what she wants is exactly what I want to give to her."

Blair's skin prickled. The gap between them had shrunk, and Madison's body was so close to hers that its heat seemed to burn her. Madison's face was so close that Blair could feel the other woman's warm breath on her cheek. She could smell the wine on Madison's lips, mingling with the scent of her hair and neck.

"Tell me." Madison spoke into Blair's ear. "What do you want, Blair?"

Blair looked into Madison's eyes. Lust stormed within them.

"You," she said. "I want you."

Madison brought her hand up to Blair's cheek, tilting Blair's head toward hers, and pressed her lips to Blair's in a hungry, blistering kiss.

At once, Blair fell apart.

CHAPTER 5

Madison snaked her hand up the back of Blair's head, kissing her harder. She slid the other arm around Blair's waist, pulling her in close. She'd been dying to kiss Blair from the moment Blair had slipped that bottle of wine between her lips.

It was madness. They were trapped together in what should have been Madison's worst nightmare. But she didn't care. She wanted Blair.

And she always got what she wanted.

A soft moan emerged from Blair's lips, filling Madison's mouth. Desire flickered through her. Blair's sweet, sultry voice echoed in Madison's mind. *I want you.* Madison wanted her too.

Suddenly, there was a loud clunk. Madison jerked back, her eyes flying open.

She blinked, then blinked again. She couldn't see anything.

The lights had gone out.

Madison froze. Her heart started to pound, her body

stiffening as she plunged back in her nightmare, unable to escape—

A sharp whirring sound came from above them. The lights flickered back on, the elevator panel lighting up.

Blair looked around. "Is the elevator fixed?"

They waited. But the elevator didn't move. Madison stood, ignoring her body's protests from sitting down for so long, and went over to the elevator control panel. She pushed the button for the ground floor.

But the elevator didn't move.

She began hammering the emergency call button again, her temper splintering. Nothing, just like before. She cursed. For a moment, she'd thought they were finally getting out of here. But she was still trapped in this stupid box.

She sat back down and slumped against the wall, her hopes dashed. What if they were going to be stuck in here all night?

Blair put her hand on Madison's. "How are you doing?"

"I'm fine," Madison said. "I thought for a moment that we were getting out of here."

"Me too. I'm sure it won't be that long. We'll just have to hang in here."

The elevator fell silent. It was hard to believe that just a moment ago, they'd been making out like teenagers. The madness that had possessed Madison had passed, reality settling in its wake. They were stuck in this box with no escape.

But Madison had been in this situation before. She'd gotten through it. She could do it again.

"Are you going to be okay?" Blair asked. "Need another distraction?"

"No, it's fine. I'm all right."

Madison's initial panic from the lights going out had dissipated, although her heart still hadn't quite slowed down. Suddenly, she was exhausted. It had to be well past midnight. She'd been on her feet all day, and the stress of the past few hours began to hit.

"It's getting late," Madison said. "I'm in desperate need of sleep. That's going to be difficult in here, but I'm going to try."

"Good idea." Blair looked around. "How do you want to do this? Should we spread out a little?"

"If we stretch out diagonally, we can both lie down. It will be a little snug."

Blair smiled. "I'm okay with that if you are."

Christ. That smile of Blair's made something stir inside her, and not just because it was wickedly sexy. It was warm and contagious. Why did Blair's smile provoke such deep feelings in her? She'd only met Blair a few hours ago. And yet, Madison felt like she really knew her. She'd felt like that from the moment they'd met, and the feeling had only strengthened.

"I'm fine with that," Madison said.

They rose and pushed their bags and the bottle of wine aside, spreading their coats out on the floor once more. Then, they stretched out diagonally across the elevator, contorting to fit. Madison turned to lie on her side, facing away from Blair. They had no choice but to lie close, but Madison was attempting to maintain some propriety despite everything.

But as Madison closed her eyes and began drifting off to sleep, she felt Blair sling her arm loosely around her waist.

~

When Blair awoke, she found Madison sitting up, her back against the wall of the elevator, looking down at her.

"Madison." Slowly, it dawned on Blair that her head was in Madison's lap. She sat bolt upright. She vaguely remembered shifting positions while half asleep. "How long have you been awake?"

"Not long," Madison replied.

"You should have woken me up so you'd have someone to talk to."

"I didn't want to disturb you. And I'm a grown woman. I can survive a few minutes without you." Madison gave her a soft smile. "Besides, having you here with me is enough to keep me calm."

Blair returned her smile. "Having you here is helpful for me too. I'm not even claustrophobic, but I don't know what I'd have done if I was all alone in here. Or worse, if I was stuck in here with some stranger."

Too late, Blair realized what she'd said. She glanced at Madison. Had Madison picked up on it? Was she aware that they weren't quite strangers? Of course, Blair could just tell her, but now she felt awkward about not having said it earlier.

But Madison didn't seem to notice. "We may have been strangers at first, but we're certainly not strangers anymore."

Madison reached behind her head and pulled the elastic

band from her hair, freeing it from its bun. "That's better." Drawing her fingers through her cinnamon brown locks, she shook them out so they cascaded down her back. "You know, our date was cut short. And just when things were getting interesting. How about we continue getting to know each other?"

Blair's stomach fluttered. She'd been wondering if that kiss had just been a crazy dream. "Sure. I'd like that."

Madison's gaze flicked to the corner of the elevator where the bottle of wine sat. She picked it up and offered it to Blair. "More wine?"

"Are you trying to get me drunk?" With the way Blair was behaving, she might as well have been drunk already.

"Definitely not. I want you to have all your wits about you."

Blair took a sip of the wine and passed the bottle back to Madison. "Are we planning to do something that will require me to have my wits?"

Madison's eyebrow quirked up. "You ask a lot of questions."

"I thought you liked a determined woman."

"I do. But there comes a point where I like an obedient woman even more." She gave Blair a pointed look. "And I'd say we've gotten to that point, wouldn't you?"

Blair didn't respond. She wanted to pretend that she still had some control over herself. She wanted to pretend that she wasn't entirely under Madison's spell. She wanted to pretend that she wasn't helpless in the face of her rapidly growing desires.

But with the way Madison was looking at her, it was hopeless.

Blair bit her lip. "I just have one more question for you. It's an important one. It's about Mistress."

Madison raised an eyebrow. "You're still trying to interview me? After everything?"

"This isn't for the interview. It's personal."

"All right. You can ask me one more question. Choose wisely."

"My question is about the Mistress name. I know you already gave me an answer, but is that really all it is?" Blair hesitated. "I've heard things. Rumors, from other women, about you."

"Oh? What kind of rumors?" There was a hint of amusement in Madison's voice.

"They're about your... unusual tastes in bed. Not that I'm implying you sleep with lots of women," Blair said quickly. "Not that there would be anything wrong with that if you did."

Madison chuckled. "None of the women in this city can keep their mouths shut, can they? All right. Here's what's really behind the Mistress name. Everything I told you is true. We chose the name because it gelled with the company's mission statement." She gave Blair an enigmatic look. "But that's not the only reason. The four of us who run Mistress, we were friends before we started the company, but it wasn't because we went to Moore University. We're all members of an exclusive club in town. A BDSM club. It was there that we formed our strong friendships. And when I decided to start Mistress, my friends were the first people I asked to help me out. The name is a tribute to that. To what we all have in common."

So the rumors were true. Not that Blair really needed

confirmation. The past few hours had made it abundantly clear that Madison didn't leave her dominant personality at the bedroom door.

Blair twirled a strand of hair around her finger. "I have another question."

"I don't think so," Madison said. "We had an agreement."

"I know. But this is related to my first question. It's important." Blair gave her an innocent look. "Please?"

Madison narrowed her eyes. "You're lucky that I find you irresistible. Usually, I'm firm when it comes to my word."

Blair smiled. "I think you're going to like this question."

"Fine. Go ahead."

Blair drew in a breath. "Will you show me why there are all those rumors about you?"

CHAPTER 6

At first, Madison didn't respond. She stared back at Blair, an inscrutable expression on her face.

Finally, she spoke. "You have no idea how much I've enjoyed unraveling you tonight." Her voice fell to a whisper. "Now, I'm going to make you come apart completely."

Blair let out a shallow breath. This was officially the wildest thing she'd ever done. But over the last few hours, her inhibitions had simply melted away.

All that was left was pure, unrestrained lust.

Madison drew close, letting her lips brush Blair's cheek. "Remember how I said I like to torture women with pleasure? You're about to get a taste of that." She pulled back. "But only if you can behave yourself. Only if you obey me. Can you do that?"

Blair nodded, desire pulsing inside her.

"Hold on to the handrail above you."

Blair shifted so her back was against the wall and raised her arms to grab onto the handrail.

"Do not let go," Madison said. "If you do, I'll have to

come up with a more creative way to keep you holding on. Almost anything can be made into a rope."

The idea of being tied up by Madison sent a thrill through Blair's body. Nevertheless, she brought her hands together above her, gripping the rail even tighter.

Slowly, Madison leaned in and pressed her lips against Blair's. Blair closed her eyes, sinking into the kiss. It was soft, restrained, less desperate than the last kiss they'd shared. But it made Blair want to crumble all the same.

Madison deepened the kiss, her hands wandering down Blair's sides, her breasts pushing against Blair's chest. Blair's arms twitched with the urge to touch Madison in return. But Madison had made herself very clear. Blair wasn't to let go. Blair wasn't to touch.

She wasn't to do anything but endure Madison's exquisite torment.

Madison broke away. Blair's lips tried to follow, but her arms held her in place.

"Impatient, are we?" Madison crooned. "Just give me a few moments and you'll be getting my full attention."

Madison slid her hands into the waist of Blair's skirt, pulling out her blouse. She tugged it up past Blair's shoulders and head, leaving it gathered around her upraised arms. The stretchy blouse was tight around Blair's forearms, binding them together.

All she had to do was let go of the handrail and she'd be free. But freedom was the furthest thing from Blair's mind.

Madison drew her fingers down Blair's cheek, tracing a line down the side of her throat and between her breasts. "There's so much I could show you if we weren't trapped in here."

Madison's other hand roamed up the front of Blair's leg, up past her knee and underneath her skirt. Blair blew a strand of hair out of her face, her head tipping back against the wall. She must have looked like a mess. She was hot and sweaty, her hair in disarray, her clothing rumpled from her short nap. But she didn't care.

And judging by Madison's ravenous stare, Madison didn't care either. "If we were back in my apartment, in my bed, I'd tie those hands of yours so you wouldn't be able to do a single thing while I played with you. You'd look so delectable trussed up for me."

She slipped her fingertips into the cup of Blair's bra and pulled it down, baring a breast. She swept her fingers over the nipple until it turned into a hard peak, then pinched it gently. Blair let out a sharp sigh.

Under Blair's skirt, Madison slid her hand further up the inside of Blair's thigh. "After tying you up, I'd blindfold you. Then you'd have no choice but to focus on me alone."

Madison's hand crept up to the juncture of Blair's thighs. She ran her fingertips up Blair's panties, pressing them hard into her slit. Blair trembled, heat flooding her. She tried to part her legs, but her skirt was too tight. Still holding on to the rail, she wriggled her hips, attempting to work the skirt further up her thighs.

Madison spoke into her ear again. "Then, I'd spank you, over and over, until your skin was on fire and you'd beg me to soothe the ache within."

Blair quivered. She could feel the warmth of Madison's cheek next to hers and could smell the scent of her. Blair wanted to kiss Madison, to tear off her skirt and panties so she could feel Madison's fingers against her. But one thing was clear—Madison was running the show. So Blair held back.

"Unfortunately, we're stuck in here, without a rope or a paddle in sight." Madison pulled away. "I'll have to find other ways to torture you."

Blair forced herself to wait patiently, anticipation burning inside. Madison skimmed her hands up the sides of Blair's thighs, pushing her skirt up past her hips, then took the waistband of Blair's panties. Blair lifted her hips, urging Madison to yank her panties down.

But Madison took her time, peeling them from Blair's legs, inch by painstaking inch. Finally, she tossed them aside. Blair's heart began to race. With her bra half off, her panties gone, and her hands restrained, she felt exposed. Her entire body was alight, her arms beginning to tingle. She squeezed and flexed them, but she didn't let go of the railing.

"Still holding on?" Madison asked. "You're much more obedient than I expected. Most women like you have a hard time letting go." She let her fingers linger at Blair's breasts while dragging her other hand down Blair's stomach. "But not you. Your body is begging for surrender. I can feel it."

Blair blew out a hard breath. Madison was right. Blair needed Madison with every part of her being. She would beg if she had to. She'd never had such a thought in her life. She'd always liked it when the other woman took control during sex, but this was something else entirely. She didn't just want Madison to take control.

She wanted to lose herself to Madison completely.

Madison slipped a finger between Blair's thighs, pushing it into her slit. Blair exhaled sharply, pleasure lancing through her. She lifted her hips, pushing back against the other woman, her grip on the railing above her tightening.

Madison pulled back. "Uh uh. You said you wanted me to show you why there are all those rumors about me and my tastes. For me to do that, you need to let me have command of your body. Any pleasure you receive will be given by me, not you. So you're going sit still, close your eyes, and not do or say a single thing until I tell you to. And you're not going to come until I tell you to. Do you understand?"

Blair nodded, too overcome with need to speak.

"Good. Now, where was I?"

Madison pushed her fingers back down between Blair's lower lips, running them up and down slowly. Blair bit the inside of her cheek. It took all her energy to remain still. Each stroke of Madison's fingers fired aftershocks through her, each nudge on her clit made her gasp for air. From the moment Madison had kissed her, Blair had been throbbing. Now, that feeling was growing uncontrollably.

Finally, Madison slid a finger inside her, then another, piercing Blair to her core. A moan escaped her lips. But Madison continued to tease her, dipping in and out slowly, gliding against that sweet spot inside with every thrust. And every time, Blair's body screamed for more. Her arms strained at the blouse holding them together, her elbows locking. She was so close. She craved release. But Madison held her there, right at the edge.

She sucked air through her teeth, her body trembling. So this was what Madison meant by 'torture.' It was torture of the most heavenly kind.

For what had to be the hundredth time, Madison drew

her fingers back to graze Blair's wet folds. Blair whimpered feverishly.

"Is there something you'd like to say?" Madison asked.

Blair nodded.

"You may speak."

"I'm close," Blair said.

"I know. But I said you couldn't come unless I tell you to."

"Yes, but—" Blair squeezed her eyes shut. This was unbearable.

"If you ask nicely, I might allow it."

"Please. Please, can I come?"

Madison tilted her head to the side as if thinking hard. "But I'm having so much fun toying with you like this." She eased a finger inside Blair again, letting the base of her palm roll over her swollen nub.

A groan rose from Blair's chest.

"On the other hand, you've been such a good submissive." Madison's fingers delved into her deeper, setting off sparks inside Blair. "Perhaps you've earned your release."

A tremor rocked Blair's body, her hands almost slipping from the handrail above her.

"All right," Madison said. "Come."

At once, pleasure erupted deep within her, rippling through her body. A primal cry flew from her lips. When Blair couldn't take any more, Madison eased off and planted a blazing, lust-filled kiss on her lips.

As Blair started to wonder how long she could survive without coming up for air, Madison broke the kiss, an amused smile on her face. "You're still holding on. I'm impressed."

Blair looked up at her arms. Somehow, they remained locked to the handrail.

"That's good. I'm not done with you yet." Madison drew her thumb along the curve of Blair's jaw. "You see, I'm not the type of Mistress focused solely on my submissive's pleasure. I expect to be repaid for all my hard work. To be thanked for giving you that earth-shattering orgasm. To be praised and worshiped, to have you bow before me. Do you want to repay me, Blair?"

Blair nodded. "Anything, Mistress."

Madison stood up. "You can let go."

Blair released the handrail and lowered her arms. They were still twisted in her blouse. Madison tugged it from Blair's arms, freeing her. Blood rushed to her hands, sending pins and needles through them. Her whole body tingled pleasantly.

Madison leaned back against the wall and pointed to the floor before her. "Get on your knees."

Blair positioned herself so she was kneeling at Madison's feet. Madison towered above her, her long, smooth legs stretching up above Blair. Madison took the hem of her dress and hiked it up around her waist. Underneath, she wore a pair of silky black panties with lace accents. Inside Blair, desire flickered to life again.

Madison looked down at her. Without taking her eyes off Blair, she slipped her fingers into her panties and pushed them down her hips. "It's time for you to repay me." She kicked her panties aside. "I'm sure you know what to do."

Madison parted her legs. Blair moved closer to Madison until she was right underneath her and ran her hand up the inside of Madison's thigh. She did the same to Madison's other leg with her lips, kissing her way up it. Madison spread her feet further apart, urging Blair on.

Blair dragged her lips up to the apex of Madison's thighs, brushing them over Madison's lower lips. She took a moment to savor the liquid heat that covered them, before parting them with the tip of her tongue.

Madison's body hitched. She grabbed hold of the railing at either side of her, anchoring herself as she arched out toward Blair. Blair drew her tongue up to probe at Madison's clit, eliciting a soft hiss from her. Blair pursed her lips around it, sucking gently.

A string of curses fell from Madison's mouth. It was so delightfully unexpected. Clearly, Blair was doing something right. She grabbed onto Madison's hips to brace herself as she redoubled her efforts, sucking and licking and flicking, feeling Madison's body react to her touch.

"Oh, Blair…" Madison's hands dropped to Blair's head. Her fingers tangled in Blair's hair as she clutched Blair to her.

Blair continued, coaxing unbridled cries from Madison's body with every flicker of her tongue. It only took a few more seconds for Madison to come undone. Her grip on Blair's hair tightened, her shuddering scream filling the elevator as she rode out her pleasure.

Once Madison's body calmed, Blair planted a gentle kiss at the peak of Madison's thighs, letting her fingers trail down the other woman's legs. After a few moments, Madison slid down to the floor, settling herself beside Blair.

Madison ran a hand through her hair from back to front, pushing it out of her flushed face. "Christ, that was intense."

"I could say the same thing," Blair replied.

"Did that answer your question, then?"

Blair smiled. "Definitely."

Madison took Blair's cheek in her palm. "For the record, most of those rumors about me are just rumors. I'm not the type to do this with just anyone. It takes a remarkable woman to bring that out in me."

Blair looked back into Madison's eyes. There was a softness in them that Blair hadn't seen all night. Madison kissed her softly before taking Blair in her arms and tossing her coat over them like a blanket.

Blair closed her eyes with a sigh. But as she did, the thought she'd pushed to the back of her mind began to grow. There was something she'd kept from Madison.

And Blair needed to tell her the truth.

CHAPTER 7

Blair untangled herself from Madison's arms. They'd both dozed off again. Trying her hardest not to wake the other woman, Blair grabbed her panties and slipped them back on before fixing the rest of her clothes. The last thing she wanted was for someone to come along and rescue them, only to find her in a state of undress. That this hadn't occurred to Blair earlier, when Madison had been doing all kinds of dirty things to her, proved the rashness of their actions.

That didn't stop Blair from returning to Madison's side and snuggling up against her again.

A moment later, Madison's eyes fluttered open.

Blair gave her a lazy smile. "Morning."

"Good morning." Madison looked at her watch, yawning.

"What time is it?" Blair's phone had run out of battery.

"Just past 2 a.m."

Too late, Blair realized that drawing attention to the

time might set off Madison's panic again. But she didn't seem too concerned.

Blair glanced sideways at her. Perhaps now was a good time to come clean.

Madison frowned. "What is it?"

It was now or never. "There's something I should tell you." Blair paused. "You were right."

"About what?"

"About why I wanted to interview you. It wasn't just because of the assignment. I didn't say anything because it feels a little silly, but…" Blair hesitated. "I didn't just want to interview you. I wanted to see you. Again."

"Again?" Madison pressed her lips together in thought. "So we *have* met before." It was a statement, not a question.

"You don't sound surprised."

"When you introduced yourself to me outside my office, I thought you looked familiar, but I couldn't place you. I usually don't forget a face."

"It was years ago. And we only met briefly."

"Where did we meet?" Madison asked.

"At Moore U. I was in my freshman year. I'd just moved to the city. I'd lived most of my life in this small town, with this conservative family. Growing up, I felt like I never really fit in. I never felt like I belonged anywhere. It was hard. I worked for years after high school so I could afford to move away, to come here to the city and go to college. I wanted to find a place where I could really be myself, where I could embrace the parts of myself that I'd had to keep buried."

Blair didn't go into detail. She didn't need to. She was

sure that even Madison had felt like that at some point in her life, just like every other woman like them.

"But when I got here, I just felt so out of my depth," Blair said. "I had no idea what I was doing. I thought I'd made a huge mistake. I felt so lost like I didn't belong at all. And then… I met you."

Blair looked at Madison, but her face was still blank. "It was at some function the journalism department held. Women in Journalism, I think. You were one of the speakers. You'd just started Mistress, but it was really taking off. I was so in awe of you the whole time you were speaking. This incredible, commanding, successful woman, who completely owned everything about herself, including her sexuality. You were everything I wanted to be."

Blair stopped short. She didn't mean to sound so fawning, but back then, she'd been starstruck by Madison. "After the event, we got the chance to network. I gathered all my courage and went over and spoke to you. It was only for ten minutes or so. But for that ten minutes, it was just the two of us. And the conversation we had, it made me feel like I could find my way in the world. That I could become the person I wanted to be, live my life I dreamed of living, just like you. And I never forgot that. I never forgot you."

For a moment, Madison was silent. Then she spoke quietly. "I remember. I remember you now. That soft-spoken redheaded who so boldly came up to speak to me."

"I was nervous as hell."

"I barely noticed." A slow, slight smile formed on Madison's face. "Even then, something about you commanded my attention. I remember wishing I could speak to you for longer. For a fleeting moment, I considered asking you to get a drink with me, so we could talk some more, but it would have been wholly unprofessional."

"I think I would have fainted if you'd asked me for a drink back then," Blair said. "I had a bit of a crush on you. But I've outgrown it since then." That wasn't quite true. "What I mean is, that's not why I wanted to interview you. I just wanted to see you again, if for no reason other than to prove to myself how far I've come."

"You have come a long way. You're far surer of yourself now than you were that night. The woman I met that night wouldn't have faced off to me in my office and demanded I let her interview me."

"That's true. I can hardly believe I did that even now."

Madison stretched out her arms and wrapped them around Blair again. "This explains so much. All this time, I've been feeling like I knew you somehow, but I couldn't remember who you were. I'm glad I agreed to let you interview me."

A thought occurred to Blair. If she hadn't stopped Madison in front of the reception desk earlier in the night, would the two of them have ended up stuck on this broken-down elevator? If they hadn't gotten stuck on this elevator, would Blair have ever gotten to speak to Madison again?

Would anything have happened between them at all?

Blair didn't dare give voice to her thoughts. She didn't want to ruin things.

"There's something else I've been wondering about," Madison said. "Earlier on, when I was having a panic attack. How did you know how to handle it?"

Blair shrugged. "I didn't know how to handle it. I just did what felt right. Was it the right thing to do?"

"It worked, so yes. To be honest, I've never had a panic attack with anyone else around. I haven't had one in a long time, but in the past, I'd never let anyone see me like that. I kept them secret. I kept everything secret."

Madison's eyes grew distant, like she was struggling with something in her mind. What was it?

She looked at Blair. "If I tell you something, will you promise to keep it private?"

"Of course," Blair said. "This is all off the record."

∽

Madison stretched her legs out in front of her, crossing them at the ankles as she gathered her thoughts. Beside her, Blair waited silently for her to continue.

"You asked me earlier, what motivated me to start Mistress," Madison said. "I said that I wanted to give people a voice. Women in particular. But what made me realize that is a far longer story."

It had been a long time since Madison had revisited the incident that had split her life into 'before' and 'after'. But current events had forced it to the forefront of her mind, and suddenly, talking about it didn't seem like such a difficult prospect.

"When I was in my mid-twenties, I took some time off to travel around Europe," she said. "I was feeling restless with my life. I felt like something was missing, but I didn't know what it was."

Madison almost laughed every time she thought about it. Dropping everything to go to a foreign country to 'find herself' was such a cliché, but that had been the kind of person Madison was back then. Idealistic. Privileged. Innocent.

"I was backpacking across Eastern Europe solo, visiting areas that were off the beaten track," she said. "I met a young man, a local. We were going in the same direction, so he generously offered to act as a guide. We ended up traveling together for days.

"Then one afternoon, he directed me onto a minibus that was supposed to take us to a nearby town. I didn't notice at the time that the only other passengers were a group of rough-looking men. Eventually, the bus stopped in the middle of nowhere and one of the men got out a gun. They tied up my wrists and forced me into the back of a van. It was a kidnapping."

Madison glanced at Blair. There was a hint of shock on her face, but she didn't say anything. Madison was grateful for that. She didn't want sympathy from Blair. It was hard for her not to see sympathy as pity.

"I didn't know that at a time," she said. "The men, they didn't tell me what they were doing or where they were taking me. They simply told me they wouldn't hurt me if I cooperated. In hindsight, they kept me in the dark intentionally to keep me compliant. It worked. For all I knew, they were going to kill me. I was terrified."

Her stomach churned, the memories of that moment filling her head. "I was taken to a secluded house and to a room beneath it, a cellar. It was the size of a small bedroom, but it had no windows, no light coming in at all. It seemed so much smaller. It felt so much smaller."

Understanding dawned on Blair's face. "That's why you don't like small spaces."

Madison nodded. Up until a couple of years ago, her claustrophobia had been overwhelming. She'd built her life around it, avoiding enclosed spaces and moving into a huge, open-plan apartment. It was why there was so much glass in the Mistress offices. Having solid walls around her had once made her too anxious. It wasn't much of a problem for her anymore. At least, it hadn't been, until now.

Madison took a deep breath and continued. "The kidnappers locked me in there without a word. It wasn't until after I was freed that I learned why they'd taken me. They'd simply wanted a ransom. The man I was traveling with had criminal connections. He'd deduced from what I'd told him about myself that I wasn't just any American tourist. He'd looked me up, realized how wealthy my family was, and he saw an opportunity there.

"They contacted my father, told him they had me and that they'd release me if he sent them money. My father agreed to pay. The amount they were asking for was nothing to him. But getting it together and transferring it to the kidnappers took time. Two days, to be exact. They held me for two days, but it felt so much longer." Madison's voice faltered. "It was not knowing that was the worst. If they'd only told me why they'd taken me, it would have made everything more bearable."

"Oh, Madison." It seemed Blair couldn't hold any longer. "That must have been awful for you."

"It was a nightmare," Madison said. "And it didn't end after those two days. When my father's money finally came through, they let me go, and I ended up back home and safe. But in the aftermath of the incident, I struggled to make sense of the world. It was a difficult time for me. But slowly, I began to heal.

"And when I finally did, I was changed in two major ways. The first was that I became obsessed with control. After my ordeal, after having power stripped away from me, I vowed to never be helpless again. And secondly, I found myself with a renewed sense of purpose. I'd looked into the barrel of a gun and lived. I began to feel that I survived for a reason. That I was meant to do something more than write for some traditional, conventional newspaper. I had to do something meaningful with my life. And that was when my vision of Mistress took root in my mind."

Madison turned to Blair, meeting the other woman's eyes for the first time since she began her story. "The reason I don't talk about what I went through isn't because it's difficult. It's because I don't want my story to be reduced to a moment when I had my power stripped from me. I don't want it to be seen as the defining event in my life. I'm who I am today because of my choices and actions in the present. That's what defines me."

Blair took Madison's hand. "I understand that. I really do."

Madison couldn't help but smile back at her. It felt good to open up to Blair. There was just something about her that made Madison feel at ease. "Blair, when we get out of here," she began, "I—"

Suddenly, the elevator clanged and jerked. The lights flickered. Blair's hand tightened around Madison's.

The elevator began to fall.

CHAPTER 8

Blair's pulse hammered in her ears. She clung to Madison's hand as the elevator dropped.

But it didn't plunge to the ground. Instead, it continued in a steady, controlled descent.

"The elevator," Blair said. "It must be fixed."

"We're finally getting out of here." The relief was clear in Madison's voice.

Blair looked at the display above the elevator door. It was counting down the floors. Soon they would reach ground level. Her stomach stirred. She was relieved, although probably not as relieved as Madison. But at the same time, she felt the faintest tug of disappointment. Once they were out of here, she and Madison would go their separate ways.

Blair pushed the feeling aside and stood up on shaky legs. All that mattered was that they were moments from freedom.

The elevator reached the ground floor and stopped with

a shudder. Blair held her breath. The seconds stretched out, until finally, the doors slid open.

Blair shielded her eyes, blinking against the harsh fluorescent lights of the lobby.

"Go on," Madison said. "After you."

Blair stepped out of the elevator, Madison at her heels. As her vision adjusted to the light, she saw that the lobby was filled with people. EMTs. Firefighters. Security.

A dark-haired woman pushed through the gathered crowd and hurried toward them, her face warped with concern. She pulled Madison into a hug. "Are you okay? This must have been awful for you."

"I'm fine, Yvonne," Madison replied.

Once again, Blair's research was paying off. The dark-haired woman was Yvonne Maxwell, the second in command at Mistress Media.

"Excuse me, ma'am?" An EMT stood before them. "We need to take a look at you. Just to make sure you're okay." He gestured toward a bench to the side where another EMT was setting up her gear.

Blair and Madison sat down on the bench. Yvonne hovered by Madison, fussing over her until one of the EMTs told her to give them some space. Someone wrapped Blair in a blanket and handed her a bottle of water. But Blair wasn't cold or thirsty. Being suddenly surrounded by people was overwhelming.

As the EMT took Blair's blood pressure, a man in a suit walked over to them, an apologetic expression on his face. "Ms. Sloane, I'm from building management. I'd like to extend an apology to you both. I'm sorry this happened."

"What exactly did happen?" Madison asked firmly. "How

did we end up stuck in there? Why did it take so long to get us out?"

"It took some time for anyone to figure out what was going on. Maintenance got the emergency call from the elevator, but when they answered, they couldn't hear anything."

"We couldn't hear anything either," Madison said.

"We figured there was a problem with the intercom, but we assumed someone was in there, we just couldn't speak to you. We were working on the problem from the beginning. It was an electrical malfunction. Rest assured, you were never in any danger."

Beside them, Yvonne scoffed. "Never in any danger? They were trapped for hours!"

The man shot Yvonne an irritated look. "As I told you earlier, they were perfectly safe the entire time." He turned back to Blair and Madison. "All the safety features were fully functional. It was just a matter of getting you out. We were preparing to send someone up the shaft, but our engineers managed to fix the problem ten minutes ago."

"It certainly took long enough," Yvonne said. "I told them to send someone up there hours ago, but no one would listen to me."

"As I told you, it was a last resort." His weary scowl made it clear that Yvonne had been hounding him for some time now.

"All that matters is that we're out now." Madison nodded politely to the man. "Thank you for taking care of the situation. We'll discuss it further on Monday."

The man scurried away, clearly relieved to have escaped further scrutiny. As the EMTs continued to check Blair and

Madison over, Yvonne filled Madison in on everything that had happened.

"Everyone's been so worried," she said. "When you didn't show up for dinner, I called around. I got hold of the receptionist and she said you'd left the office an hour earlier. She also mentioned there was an issue with one of the building's elevators. I put two and two together and came here as quickly as I could. I've been waiting for you since. Are you sure you're all right?"

"I'm fine, really. It was a little stressful, but I wasn't alone." Madison turned to Blair. "Blair, this is my friend Yvonne. Yvonne, this is Blair Chase. She's a journalism student. She came into the office to interview me and had the good fortune of ending up stuck in the elevator too."

Yvonne held out her hand for Blair to shake. "Sorry we couldn't meet under better circumstances. Thank you for keeping Madison company."

Blair shook Yvonne's hand. Normally, she would have been almost as awestruck at meeting a woman like Yvonne Maxwell as she'd been when meeting Madison for the first time. But after the whirlwind night Blair had just had, this didn't even register.

Beside them, the EMT cleared her throat. "You're both completely fine. No signs of dehydration or shock. In situations like these, I usually recommend that you go to the hospital to be assessed more thoroughly, but I don't think that's necessary. A few hours rest will do you better than sitting around in a hospital waiting room."

Rest sounded great. Blair's exhaustion was hitting her hard now.

"Just make sure to take care of yourselves over the next

couple of days. And if you experience any unusual symptoms, don't hesitate to go see a doctor. Even psychological symptoms. Going through something like this can be stressful."

Blair nodded.

"You're free to go." The EMT began packing up her things.

So this was it. Blair glanced at Madison, trying unsuccessfully to catch her eye. She felt a heaviness in her chest. Out here in the vast lobby, surrounded by people, she and Madison were a world apart, like they had been before they'd stepped into the elevator.

"I have a car waiting," Yvonne told Madison. "Only the one. I didn't know there was anyone else in there with you." She turned to Blair. "I can call another for you, or we can drop you off."

"It's okay, I can get home myself." Although Blair wasn't sure how she'd do that considering her phone had run out of battery.

"Nonsense," Madison said. "We're dropping you off. It's the least I can do, considering the reason you ended up in this mess is because I was running late. Where do you live?"

"West Heights. It's probably out of the way for you." Blair didn't know where Madison lived, but she doubted it was anywhere near the rundown part of the city Blair lived in.

"It's fine. I want to see that you get home safely. What's the address?"

Blair gave Madison the address. Somehow, she dragged herself out of the building. There was a black car waiting for them with a driver standing by. Madison urged Blair into the back seat and slid in next to her. Yvonne got into the front.

The car ride was spent in silence. Blair was too tired to speak. And now that she and Madison were out in the real world, it was like Madison was a stranger to her. Had everything that had passed between them in the elevator really happened? Had it all been the result of temporary madness?

Was everything they'd shared meaningless now?

The car pulled up out the front of Blair's apartment.

Blair looked at Madison. "This is me."

"Are you going to be all right?" Madison asked. "You shouldn't be alone after something like that. Will you have anyone with you?"

"My roommate should be home," Blair said.

"Be sure to let her know what happened. Like the EMT said, it was quite an ordeal we went through. You should have someone with you, just in case."

Blair nodded. Beside her, the driver opened the door. Blair unbuckled her seatbelt. "I'll get going, then."

Madison placed her hand on Blair's forearm. "Wait."

Blair's voice caught in her throat. "Yes?"

"Your assignment. Did you get enough material to write the article?"

Blair blinked. She'd forgotten all about it. "I think so."

"Good. I'd feel awful if all this was for nothing." Madison reached into her briefcase and produced a small white card and a pen. "Let me give you my details. If you have any more questions, feel free to get in touch."

She scribbled on the card, then handed it to Blair. It was Madison's business card. On the back, Madison's cell number was written in graceful script.

"Don't hesitate to contact me if you need anything," Madison said.

"I will." Blair slipped the card between the pages of her notebook and returned it to her purse.

"It was lovely meeting you, circumstances aside."

"Yeah. You too."

Madison gave her a farewell nod. "Goodnight, Blair."

"Goodnight."

Blair slung her bag over her shoulder and got out of the car. As she headed to the entrance of her apartment, something pulled inside her chest. With each step she took, the feeling only grew stronger.

As she reached the front steps, she turned and looked back toward the road, just in time to see the car pull away from the curb and drive off, taking Madison away with it.

CHAPTER 9

"Madison?" Yvonne said. "Are you even listening to me?"

Madison blinked. She'd been staring out the window of her office. She looked up at Yvonne, who stood before Madison's desk, glaring down at her impatiently. "Yes. You're saying we should acquire Q Magazine."

"I know it doesn't sound like a good move, with print on the way out and all. But we can turn things around if we turn it into an online-only publication. It will take a lot of capital, so I'll call Lydia and have her run the numbers, but I'm confident we can make it work."

"Sure," Madison murmured. She trusted Yvonne, and she trusted Yvonne's business instincts. They'd gotten Mistress this far.

"Speaking of Lydia, things would be so much easier if she'd come work for us. We need someone to handle the finances in-house. We should make her an offer. We're already paying her outrageous consulting fees."

As Yvonne continued, Madison tried her hardest not to

let her mind wander. She'd been unfocused all day, unable to stop thinking about the night in the elevator. Once she'd finally gotten home on Saturday morning, she'd slept until midday, enjoying the comfort of her bed, then she'd spent the whole weekend enjoying her freedom. It was Monday morning now, and yet Madison couldn't stop thinking about that night.

About Blair.

Whenever Madison thought about her, she felt a yearning ache. It didn't make sense. She and Blair had just been two strangers, their previous encounter aside. Although Blair had remembered Madison vividly from years ago, to Madison, Blair had just been a woman with whom she'd had a fleeting, albeit remarkable, encounter.

And yet, it felt like Madison had known her for so much longer, each hour a decade in a lifetime. During that time, Blair had seen Madison at her most vulnerable. More importantly, Madison had let Blair in, and felt perfectly comfortable doing so. That rarely happened.

Madison shook her head. All these feelings were just a side effect of what she'd gone through with Blair. Everything that had happened between them was just due to the stress of the situation. They'd opened up to each other because they were trapped and afraid. They'd kissed out of desperation. And everything after the kiss? That was Madison trying to regain a sense of control in a situation in which she'd felt powerless.

"Madison?"

"Hm?" Madison looked up again. "Yes, sure. I'll talk to Lydia."

Yvonne examined Madison's face. "Are you all right?"

"I'm fine."

Yvonne put her hands on her hips. "No, you're not."

Madison sighed. She'd gotten through the past few days without anyone noticing anything was amiss, but she should have known she couldn't fool her closest friend.

Yvonne's usually hard expression softened. She sat down carefully on the edge of Madison's desk. "Madison, you went through something stressful the other night. That would be enough to shake anyone up, let alone someone with your history."

Yvonne was one of the few people who knew about Madison's kidnapping. Now Blair did too. Blair knew more about Madison than most people in her life, and she knew her far more intimately.

"Do you need to, you know, talk to someone?" Yvonne asked. "The EMT said that an experience like that could have lasting effects."

Madison held up her hands. "I'm fine, really. Just a little distracted."

"Well, it's clear that something is going on with you. What else could it be?"

Madison hesitated. "It's about Blair."

"The journalism student you were trapped with? What about her?"

"I've been thinking about her. How she's doing, and so on."

"Considering what you went through together, it's only natural." Yvonne frowned at her. "Still, the amount of concern you have for her is unusual. What exactly happened in that elevator?"

"I suppose you could say we bonded during our time

together." Madison didn't elaborate. "But it was only because we didn't have a choice."

Yvonne scoffed. "I don't think so. In a situation like that, I'd probably be at the other person's throat. Most people would end up getting on each other's nerves."

"You only say that because you're a cynic." Yvonne was always thinking the worst of people.

"No, I say that because I'm a realist." Yvonne crossed her arms. "Throw a person into a crucible, and nine times out of ten, they break. Throw two people in a high-pressure situation together, and the same is true. If you and this woman went into an experience like that and came out the other end in one piece, that's really saying something."

Madison gave Yvonne a noncommittal murmur.

"On top of that, you were able to survive being trapped in an elevator practically unscathed. Madison, there was a time when you couldn't stand to be in a car for too long." Yvonne gestured at the glass walls around them. "You even designed the Mistress offices around your claustrophobia. I know you've come a long way since then, but would you have been able to get through all those hours stuck in a tiny space without Blair?"

"Probably not," Madison admitted.

"There you go. You shouldn't dismiss what the two of you went through together. If you're so worried about her, you should talk to her. Perhaps you've found a lifelong friend in her."

Friend. Madison hadn't told Yvonne or anyone else what had happened in the elevator between her and Blair. Not only because she wasn't the type to gossip about her sexual encounters, but also because she was struggling to accept that it had been real. Now, the passionate night they'd shared seemed like a distant dream.

Madison sighed. "I was thinking of getting in touch with her about her article. I'll reach out to her." She folded her hands in front of her. "Now, back to the acquisition."

∽

Blair held down the backspace key on her laptop, erasing the opening paragraph she'd spent the last half hour meticulously crafting. It was her twelfth attempt at starting the article. Usually, writing was easy for her. All she had to do was sit down, put her fingers to the keyboard, and the story would simply flow.

But today it was like every word had to be dragged out of her skull. And none of those words were good.

She stretched out in her chair and yawned. Was it the stress of her Friday night that was causing her writer's block? That wasn't likely. She felt fine otherwise. Perhaps it had to do with the subject of the article. Madison Sloane, journalist, CEO, billionaire, visionary.

The woman Blair had spent an incredible night with.

If Blair could go back in time and change things so that she'd never gotten trapped in that elevator with Madison, she wouldn't. She'd gladly live that night over again, just so she could see Madison. Now, in the light of day, it all seemed like an impossible fantasy.

Absently, Blair picked her notebook up from her desk and began flipping through it. As she did, a business card fell out. Madison's business card. Blair picked it up and traced her fingers over Madison's handwritten cell number.

She'd told Blair to call if she needed anything. Blair didn't *need* anything. She *wanted* something. She wanted Madison. They'd spent what had felt like an eternity together, just the two of them in their own little world. From the moment they'd parted ways, Madison's absence had felt like a void in Blair's chest. Blair wanted to call her, just to hear her voice again. No, she wanted more than that. Blair wanted to touch her, to hold her, to kiss her, just like she had in the elevator.

Blair shook her head. This was Madison Sloane she was thinking about. A woman like her would never be interested in a broke college student like Blair. Not in the real world.

She placed Madison's business card to the side and began her thirteenth attempt at the article.

Half an hour later she'd written a few passable paragraphs, but they were clinical and dry. What she'd written wasn't engaging. It wasn't moving. It wasn't good enough.

Blair should have been able to do better. That night in the elevator, she'd achieved her original goal of getting to know the woman behind Mistress Media. She'd peeled back Madison's layers, learned about her dreams and fears. Blair had discovered the passionate, driven woman that Madison was. Blair would never dream of disclosing any of the details Madison had shared with her in confidence. But if Blair was really a good writer, she should have been able to use words to paint a portrait of who Madison really was without needing to reveal a single thing.

Blair deleted everything she'd written and shut her laptop. She needed a break. She picked up her phone, which she'd silenced while she was writing. Her notifications had piled up. She had several emails.

One of them was from Madison.

Her heart stopped. She opened the message.

I trust that you've recovered from the other night. I want to read your article. Let me know when it's done so I can have a look.

Excitement and panic overtook her in equal amounts. Madison Sloane wanted to read Blair's article?

No, not *Madison Sloane*. Madison, the woman Blair had gotten to know so deeply. Blair knew her. She wasn't a stranger.

Blair steeled herself. She could do this. She would write the perfect article. She would show it to Madison. She was going to prove to herself, and to Madison, that the connection they shared was real.

CHAPTER 10

Madison entered the conference room and greeted the man and woman sitting across the table from Yvonne. They were the Taiwanese investors Madison had planned to meet for dinner on that fateful Friday night.

"Thank you for coming in." She took a seat next to Yvonne, placing the folder she held on the table before her along with her cell phone. "I apologize for Friday night."

Madison explained to the investors why she'd missed dinner. They smiled and nodded, clearly confused. The pair spoke passable English, but it was obvious that Madison's explanation of the unlikely situation she'd found herself in on Friday night was getting lost in translation. Yvonne attempted to clarify things with her rudimentary Mandarin, which appeared to help.

Once everyone was settled in, Madison opened her folder. "Let's begin. I've put together some projections…"

She glanced down at her cell phone. The screen had lit up.

It was Blair. Blair was calling.

"Madison?" Yvonne said. "You were saying?"

Madison looked up. "My apologies. I have to take this call. I'll be right back. Yvonne, you can start things off in the meantime."

Yvonne gave her an irritated glare. This was the second time Madison had snubbed these investors, although the first time it hadn't been her fault. Yvonne had stressed how important this meeting was to Madison several times over the past few days. It was clear she wasn't happy. Madison would make up for it later.

Right now, she had something far more important to deal with.

Madison strode out of the room and picked up the call. "Blair. It's good to hear from you."

"Hi, Madison." Blair's voice sounded hesitant.

"How are you?"

"I'm good. How are you doing?"

"I'm fine."

Seconds passed in silence. All the effortless closeness that had grown between them in the elevator was gone.

Finally, Blair spoke. "I've been working on that article. Actually, I've finished it."

"Good," Madison said. "Send it through to me."

There was a pause at the other end of the line. "I was hoping to give it to you in person."

In person? Madison pursed her lips, going over her schedule in her mind. She didn't have a spare moment all week.

But she couldn't pass up an opportunity to see Blair again.

"All right," Madison said. "Come by my office this afternoon at four."

"I'll be there." Blair sounded more confident now. "I'm looking forward to it."

Madison looked back toward the meeting room, where Yvonne was fielding questions from the pair of bewildered-looking investors. "I need to go. I'll see you soon."

Madison hung up her phone, then dialed her assistant's number. "I need you to clear my schedule from 4 p.m. today. Cancel everything. And let everybody know I'm not to be disturbed."

∽

Blair rode the elevator up to the Mistress Media offices on the top floor of the building. By coincidence, it was the same elevator she and Madison had gotten trapped in. Apparently, the malfunction had been fixed, but Blair held her breath for almost the entire elevator ride.

However, when she stepped out of the sliding door, her nerves didn't go away.

The receptionist smiled at her. "Blair, right? I heard about what happened. It must have been a rough experience."

"It wasn't so bad." Blair pushed her nerves aside. "I'm here to see Madison."

"She's expecting you. You can go on through. Do you remember the way?"

"I do. Thanks."

She made her way back to Madison's office. As she got closer, she spotted Madison sitting behind her desk through the glass. Blair's breath caught in her chest. Just the slightest glimpse of Madison brought back everything she'd felt in that elevator, all the heat and passion. It only made her more certain that what she'd felt for Madison was real, that everything they'd shared hadn't just been a dream.

Madison looked up. Her eyes locked on to Blair's. But through the glass, it was hard to decipher her expression. Was Madison's heart racing like Blair's?

Madison rose from her desk and opened the door. "Come in, Blair."

Blair stepped into the room. Madison pressed a button by the door. Around them, the glass walls turned from transparent to opaque, blocking out the rest of the world.

They were all alone.

Madison gestured toward a couch at the side of the room. "Take a seat."

Blair sat down. Madison joined her, crossing her stockinged legs neatly.

"I've been thinking about you," Madison said. "How have you been holding up since the other night?"

"I've been fine," Blair replied. "A good night's sleep was all I needed. How about you?"

"Apart from being skittish around elevators, I've been fine too. And I'm sure that will pass." Madison leaned toward her. "Now, let's see this article of yours."

Blair reached into her bag and took the article out. "I should warn you, it's a little personal. There's nothing in there that wasn't explicitly said on the record, but..." She held the pages close to her chest. "I know you're a private person, but after everything that we went through, it was hard not to write something, well, intimate."

"I'm sure you did a fine job. I trust your judgment."

Reluctantly, Blair handed Madison the article. It was several pages long.

Madison scanned the title at the top of the first page. "*Madison Sloane, Laid Bare.* An interesting choice of headline."

"I thought it was attention grabbing," Blair said.

Madison didn't say anything more. Instead, she began reading the article, her face a mask of concentration. Silence filled the air. Blair's mind went into overdrive. Had she made a mistake, writing something so emotive? The article wasn't the interview-style piece she'd originally planned to write. Instead, it was a story made up of two narratives—that of the night they spent trapped together, and the story the woman who the world knew as Madison Sloane.

The article spoke of how they'd worked together to get through the night, how they'd interviewed each other to pass the time, how the situation had revealed rarely seen sides of themselves. It omitted the more sensitive details, such as Madison's claustrophobia, the kiss and everything that had followed, as well as the secrets they'd shared with each other. But it succeeded in painting an honest picture of Madison as Blair saw her.

Madison turned another page, her lips pursed. What was going through her mind? Could she sense all the passion Blair had poured onto those pages? Could she tell that every word Blair had written had been for her?

Finally, Madison reached the bottom of the last page. She placed the article on the table beside her and looked up at Blair.

Blair fidgeted with her hair. "What did you think?"

"That was one of the most incredible pieces of journalism I've ever read," Madison said. "And I'm not just saying that because it was about me."

"So, you like it?"

"I love it. You told such a gripping story. You have real talent. In fact, I'm so impressed, I'd like to offer you a job here at Mistress."

Blair's mouth fell open. "Are you serious?"

"Of course. You're almost finished with your degree. You need a job in the field. Of course, with this article in your portfolio, you could get a job anywhere you wanted, but I think Mistress will be a good fit for you. That is, if you're interested."

"Are you kidding? Working here would be a dream."

"I'll talk to Mistress's editor-in-chief. It's fortunate that I'm not very involved with the journalism side of Mistress these days, otherwise we'd have a conflict of interest on our hands."

Blair frowned. "Why would it be a conflict of interest?"

"Because I'm going to take you on that date we talked about in the elevator."

"You..." Suddenly, forming sentences of her own was too difficult for Blair to manage. "A date?"

"Yes. Although it's safe to say that we're beyond first date territory, I want to do this right." Madison took both Blair's hands in hers. "Blair, those hours we spent trapped together, they were some of the most difficult of my life. And yet, it was all worth it, because it meant that I got to know you. Everything that passed between us, it made me feel like we'd known each other for a lifetime. And when it was all over, I thought that feeling would fade away. But seeing you, reading this heartfelt article of yours—it's made me realize that I don't want to say goodbye to you again. Not for a third time."

Blair's heart skittered.

"Will you let me take you on a date?" Madison asked. "Before you answer me, you should know that this has nothing to do with the job offer. One isn't conditional on the other. You can turn either down, or both."

Blair stared into Madison's eyes, finding her voice again. "I would never dream of turning either down. Madison, I feel the same way. I want to be with you. I want to see where things go between us. I want to see if what we found in that elevator can thrive out here in the world. And I really believe it can. So yes. Yes, I'll come work for Mistress. And yes, I'll go on a date with you."

A smile played on Madison's lips. She drew a hand up to caress Blair's cheek. "I'm going to do all those things I promised you in that elevator. I'm going to take you out and treat you to the perfect night." Her voice dropped low. "And then I'm going to show you what it means to truly be mine."

Before Blair could blink, Madison's lips were on hers, kissing her with an intensity that made Blair dizzy. Heat surged through her. Although they'd only shared a few kisses before, the taste of Madison's lips was so familiar, the touch of her hand so comforting.

Blair wrapped her arms around Madison's neck. Madison's lips grew more urgent, most demanding. Her body crashed against Blair's, pushing her back down onto the couch. Blair dissolved into her.

Madison dragged her palm up Blair's front, all the way

from her knee to her chest. Blair let out a sharp breath, her whole body burning. She dragged her fingers up the side of Madison's stockinged thigh and over the curve of her hip, grasping at her dress in a half-hearted attempt to get it off. She wanted to feel Madison's skin against hers. Blair wanted to touch her, and taste her, and immerse herself in her.

Blair pulled Madison toward her even harder. In response, Madison took Blair's wrists, pinning them to the couch at either side of Blair's head.

"I don't want to wait until our date," she whispered. "I want you now."

CHAPTER 11

Madison rose from the couch and looked down at Blair. "Don't move."

Blair nodded, her wide brown eyes brimming with anticipation. A spark went off inside Madison. She drew in a breath, holding her desire at bay. Moments like these were better savored slowly, like fine wine.

And Madison was desperate to find out how sweet Blair tasted.

Madison walked over to the coat rack by the door and took a dark cashmere scarf from it. She held it up to the light. It was too thin to be opaque, but it would do.

She returned to where Blair lay on the couch. Her eyes fixed on Blair's, Madison draped the scarf over the arm of the couch next to Blair's head. "Remember when I told you I would make you feel like you were the only woman in the world?"

"How could I forget?" Blair said softly.

"This is how I'm going to do that."

Madison unbuckled the thin belt that was cinched

around her waist and set it on the arm of the couch next to the scarf. Blair looked up at it, then back at Madison, confusion and curiosity written on her face. But she didn't question. Instead, she waited silently for Madison's command. It was clear that Blair knew Madison wanted her complete and utter submission. But did she know how much her submission drove Madison wild? Did she know how much it made Madison want her?

Did she know how difficult it was for Madison to maintain her iron grip on control when Blair looked at her the way she was looking at her now?

Nevertheless, Madison maintained her composure. "Your safeword is 'red.' Use it if you want me to stop."

Blair nodded.

Madison picked up the scarf. "Sit up."

Blair obeyed. Madison wrapped the scarf around Blair's head, not once, but twice. Doubled over, the thin fabric blocked out all light. She picked up the narrow belt. It was more for fashion than practicality, which made it the perfect tool to bind. Madison brought Blair's wrists together behind her back and looped the belt around them several times, then buckled it closed. It wasn't tight enough to constrict, but the leather was stiff enough that Blair wouldn't be able to slip from her bonds.

However, it was clear that Blair wasn't in a hurry to escape.

Madison took Blair by the shoulder. "Lie back down."

As soon as Blair's back hit the couch cushions, Madison reached down, undid the buttons of Blair's blouse and tore it open. Blair's lips parted expectantly. Madison stepped back to survey the woman laid out before her. Blair's chest rose and fell with her breaths, and her hair was spread beneath her head like a reddish-gold halo. Her cheeks were the same divine shade of crimson as her lips.

Heat flooded Madison's body. There was nothing more alluring than this. Blair, laid out before her, reduced to a puddle of lust. And with her eyes blindfolded and her wrists bound, Blair would have no choice but to give in to all that lust.

Madison planted a light kiss on Blair's lips, then kissed her way down Blair's neck. At the same time, she pushed up the cups of Blair's bra, letting Blair's perfect, pink breasts spill out. She ran her fingers over one of Blair's nipples, drawing a whimper from her. Madison dipped down and wrapped her lips around Blair's other nipple, sucking it gently.

Blair arched up. "Oh!"

Madison sucked harder, relishing the reactions she was coaxing from Blair's body. The red-haired woman was so responsive. The slightest touch made her shiver and purr in the most delicious way.

"That's it," Madison said, keeping her voice low and soft. "Just focus on me. Focus on my touch. Focus on the pleasure."

Madison ran her hand down Blair's stomach, sliding it to where Blair's thighs met. Beneath her, Blair's body hitched. Madison pressed the seam of Blair's pants between her legs. Blair pushed back against Madison's fingers. This time, Madison permitted her that freedom. She liked enthusiasm almost as much as she liked control.

Almost.

Madison spoke into Blair's ear. "That night in the

elevator made me wonder what you tasted like. Do you want me to taste you?"

"God, yes." Blair's hot breath warmed Madison's face. "*Please.*"

Blair's words unraveled the last of Madison's control. She slid her hands down to Blair's pants, her fingers fumbling with the button. Once they were undone, she tore them down Blair's legs, taking her panties with them. Madison pushed Blair's knees apart, arranging her legs so that one foot was on the floor, the other bent over the back of the couch.

"You're very flexible, aren't you?" Madison traced her fingertips up the inside of Blair's thigh. "I'm going to take full advantage of that in the future. The things I could do with you. There are so many possibilities."

Blair quivered, her breath deepening. Madison smiled. It was far too easy to get Blair worked up. Madison positioned herself between the other woman's legs and grabbed the insides of her trembling thighs. Madison was tempted to tease her for a while, to make her groan and beg again. But there would be plenty of opportunities for that later. They had all the time in the world.

Madison dipped her head down, bringing her lips to Blair's slick, velvet folds. A soft breath fell from Blair's lips. Madison drew her tongue up to Blair's tiny bud, painting light spirals around it, letting her lips wrap around it. Blair convulsed against her, her body begging for more.

As Madison licked and sucked, Blair's blissful murmurs escalated into fevered moans. Madison drank it all in. Blair's cries, her fragrance, her taste, the way her soft thighs shook under Madison's palms. It was electrifying.

"Madison," Blair said. "Oh, Madison!"

Blair rose up into Madison, her thighs tightening around Madison's ears. The sound that flew from Blair's lips made Madison wonder how well the soundproofing in her office worked. She didn't care if anyone heard them. All Madison cared about was milking as much pleasure from the woman before her as she could.

After drawing a second, more subdued orgasm from Blair, Madison swept her up and into an aching, possessive kiss. Blair's lips and tongue were soft but insistent. Her kisses had a way of going straight to Madison's head and right between her thighs.

Madison reached behind Blair's back and unbuckled the belt fastening Blair's wrists together. "I'm going to need your hands."

Blair rested her palms in her lap. "I'm all yours."

Madison looked Blair up and down, devouring her with her eyes. Blair had made no attempt to touch the blindfold or fix her disheveled clothes. Sitting on the couch with her feet together, her hands on her thighs, she was the picture of perfect obedience.

Where have you been all my life, Blair?

"Madison?" Blair's voice quivered with desire.

"I'm here." Madison reached out to remove the blindfold, before pulling back. Keeping Blair guessing was far more enjoyable. "I was simply admiring you."

That seemed to satisfy Blair. And Madison had no intention of keeping her waiting any longer. She lifted her skirt up around her hips and slipped out of her panties. Draping one arm over Blair's shoulders, she straddled Blair's lap, her knees at either side of the other woman's legs. She kissed

Blair again, her body crushing against Blair's. Blair groped at her blindly, her hands wandering down Madison's waist and hips. Her touch only made Madison want her even more.

Madison took Blair's hand and pulled it toward her, guiding it between her thighs in an unspoken command. Obediently, Blair slid her fingers between Madison's lower lips, skimming them along her slit. Madison shuddered, grinding back against her. Blair's gentle touch felt exquisite. While Madison usually liked to take things slow, her need for Blair overpowered her patience. All the yearning she'd felt toward Blair in the days since they'd parted had transformed into pure lust.

She ran the back of her hand down the side of Blair's face, her fingers brushing over the blindfold. "Blair," she whispered.

Madison didn't need to say anything more. Slowly, Blair glided her fingers down to Madison's entrance, slipping them inside. Madison quaked atop her. As Blair eased her fingers in and out, Madison grabbed hold of the back of the couch and began to rock her hips to an ever-increasing rhythm.

Madison grabbed a handful of Blair's silken hair, pulling firmly. Blair let out a tiny gasp and picked up the pace. Madison wrapped her other arm around Blair's shoulders, drawing her close, riding Blair's lap in a frenzy of passion. Blair matched Madison's movements, her sharp breaths an echo of Madison's, her chest heaving against Madison's.

It didn't take long for her pleasure to reach a peak. Madison tossed her head back and released a cry, letting ecstasy overtake her, losing herself in the woman before her.

As her orgasm subsided, Madison ripped off Blair's blindfold and cradled Blair's face in her hands. Their lips collided in a kiss. Blair sighed into her mouth, her body sinking into Madison's.

Madison never wanted to let go of her, not again. But now that they were together out in the world, there was no need to rush. Now, the two of them could explore their budding relationship freely. They could take their time to get to know each other all over again.

Madison broke away. "I had my assistant clear my schedule for the rest of the day. How about I take you on that date tonight?"

Blair smiled. "I'd love that."

EPILOGUE

"Quiet down, everyone," Gabrielle said. "It's time for the brides-to-be to open their gifts."

From her seat next to Blair, Madison spoke under her breath. "She better not have gotten us strippers."

Blair grinned. It wouldn't have been out of character for Gabrielle. Gabrielle Hall, Mistress Media's CMO and Madison's long-time friend, was the reason they were having this crazy bachelorette weekend in the first place. Although Blair hadn't cared if she had a bachelorette party or not, Madison had been against the idea entirely. But Gabrielle had insisted, and eventually Madison had given her permission to throw one, with the caveat it was a joint party for both herself and Blair.

Gabrielle had gone all out, organizing a weekend in Vegas for Madison and Blair, along with herself, Yvonne, and Amber, the other women who ran Mistress. It had been a wild couple of days, but tonight was their last night in Vegas before they returned home. They were spending it at a bar near their hotel. Blair was grateful for a relatively quiet night. She didn't care for the glitz and grandiosity of Vegas, but she was happy to have the chance to celebrate the fact that after almost two years, she was finally marrying the woman of her dreams.

Gabrielle gestured toward the small pile of gifts laid out on the table. "Go on. Open them."

"You first," Madison said to Blair. "Pick something."

Blair picked up a package at random, a box wrapped in black paper and tied with a velvet bow. It was surprisingly heavy.

Yvonne spoke up from across the table. "That one's from me."

Blair set the package on her lap and unwrapped it. Inside was a solid metal box. She undid the clasp on the lid and opened it up.

Madison peered over Blair's shoulder at the contents of the box. "Handcuffs."

"Those aren't just any handcuffs," Yvonne said. "They're the most secure handcuffs you can buy. Military-grade nickel-plated steel and said to be completely impossible to escape from. I have several pairs myself, and the claims are true. Don't lose the keys or you'll find yourself in a very sticky situation. Unless that's what you want."

She gave Blair a sly look, which was entirely disconcerting coming from the usually serious woman. Heat rose up Blair's face. She shut the box and mumbled a thank you. By now, she should have been used to this kind of thing. Over the years, Blair had heard the most scandalous stories about what Madison's friends got up to from their own mouths. They weren't at all shy about their tastes. Blair and

Madison's sex life was vanilla in comparison, which was really saying something.

Madison thanked Yvonne before picking out another gift from the table. It was a small envelope.

"It's from me," Amber said. "I thought you might appreciate something other than the usual vulgar bachelorette gifts."

Madison opened the envelope. Inside was a card and two tickets. "You got us a vacation."

"A trip to my family's island. It's very secluded, so you'll have to take the jet."

"Wow," Blair said. "That's incredible. Thanks."

Amber tossed her long blonde hair over her shoulder. "It's nothing."

Amber wasn't being modest. The gift was probably nothing to her. As the heiress to the Pryce family, Amber was loaded, even compared to Madison and all the others. In fact, they'd all flown to Vegas in Amber's private jet.

"What a thoughtful gift. Thank you, Amber." Madison turned to Blair. "We'll save it for later in the year. After the wedding. And the honeymoon."

After the wedding. Blair still couldn't quite believe she and Madison were getting married. After that night in the elevator, it had just been one whirlwind after another for Blair. Madison had taken her out on a date, and it had been everything Madison had promised and more. Dozens of dates like it had followed, and after countless days and nights spent together, they'd moved in together. Blair had taken the job at Mistress, and her career as a journalist had flourished as quickly as her relationship with Madison.

And after just a year, Madison had proposed. Blair had immediately said yes.

It had all happened so fast. But after everything they'd been through together, fast was about their speed.

Gabrielle cleared her throat. "If you two are done making eyes at each other, Lydia sent a gift too. And she apologized that she couldn't make it."

Lydia was the fifth member of the Mistress executive team, but she hadn't been with the company for long. She'd been invited to Vegas with everyone, but she'd declined, claiming she had plans. Blair wasn't surprised. She didn't know Lydia well, but she'd always seemed standoffish.

Gabrielle picked two gift bags up from the table and checked the tags on them before handing one each to Blair and Madison. "Lydia said not to show each other what's in the bags. Apparently, it's some kind of surprise."

Blair peered into her gift bag and lifted the tissue paper to find some lacy white lingerie, presumably intended for their wedding night. Mercifully, it was tasteful. Lydia had a good eye for style.

"Tell Lydia we said thank you." Madison glanced sideways at Blair. "If yours is anything like mine, I know I'm going to enjoy it." It seemed Madison's bag contained lingerie too.

"Dana and I got you a gift too," Gabrielle said. Dana was Gabrielle's girlfriend. She'd been too busy to join them in Vegas. "It's waiting for you in your suite."

Madison crossed her arms. "Gabi. Tell me you didn't get us a stripper. You promised there wouldn't be any strippers."

Gabrielle held up her hands defensively. "Don't worry, I

heard you loud and clear. We got you a gift basket from our favorite adult boutique. It was too big to bring to the bar. Besides, I didn't think you'd want to open it in public. Start waving some of those toys around, and we'd probably get kicked out."

Blair flushed. Whatever was in the gift basket had to be more risqué than handcuffs.

"Thank you, Gabrielle," Madison said. "For the gift, and the party." She looked around the table, her eyes brimming with unexpected affection. "Thank you. All of you."

"What are friends for?" Gabrielle said. "Besides, the fact that two people we love have found happiness is a great excuse for a party." Her eyes fell to the empty glasses on the table before Blair and Madison. "Now that the gifts are out of the way, the two of you need more drinks."

∼

As Gabrielle and Amber tried to catch the attention of a passing waitress, Madison spoke softly into Blair's ear. "I'm looking forward to trying out those handcuffs. We'll have to test whether they really are impossible to get out of."

For what had to be the tenth time that night, Blair's cheeks turned bright pink. Madison had spent the entire weekend teasing Blair. She simply couldn't help herself.

A waitress came waltzing over on ridiculously high heels. "What can I do for you?" She had a warm southern accent.

Amber waved her hand toward the table. "As you can see, we need more drinks. A round of margaritas." Amber had a bad habit of treating everyone like servants.

"Coming right up." The waitress looked around the table. Her eyes landed on the tacky 'bride-to-be' sashes Gabrielle had forced Madison and Blair to wear. "A joint bachelorette party? Isn't that a fun idea? There are two very lucky guys out there somewhere."

Amber let out an impatient sigh. "They're getting married to each other."

"Oh." The woman looked from Madison to Blair, apparently processing the information, before giving them a warm smile. "How nice. How did the two of you meet?"

"We got trapped in an elevator together," Blair said.

"That's certainly an interesting way to meet someone." The waitress began clearing the empty glasses from the table. "Let me tell you this. I've been married for ten years, and if I've learned anything, it's that if you can get through the tough times together, you're set for life. Getting stuck in an elevator definitely counts as tough."

"I wouldn't have it any other way." Madison slipped her hand into Blair's. "Getting stuck in that elevator with you was the single best thing that ever happened to me."

"Me too," Blair said. "I love you."

"I love you, too."

Across the table, Amber rolled her eyes.

The waitress brought her hand up to clutch her chest. "You two are too sweet. I can already tell that your marriage will be a happy one. I'll be right back with your drinks."

When the waitress returned, she was carrying a tray with another round of margaritas, along with a bottle of champagne. "It's on the house."

Madison thanked her. Amber popped the champagne and gave a moving toast to Madison and Blair. A few minutes later, they were joined by a trio of tasteful burlesque dancers who Gabrielle had arranged to put on a show for them all in a private room nearby. Madison suspected Gabrielle had hired them because she knew they were the closest thing to strippers that Madison would tolerate.

The night wore on. Although Madison and Blair limited themselves to only a few drinks, Gabrielle and Amber both got outrageously drunk. So did Yvonne, but it didn't show. She retained her dour demeanor the entire night.

Soon, midnight came and went. Before they knew it, it was almost 2 a.m.

Blair yawned. "Should we call it a night?"

"That sounds good." Madison got the attention of the others. "Ladies, Blair and I are going to turn in."

"Already?" Gabrielle asked.

"I'm not as young as all of you." Although Madison was barely any older than everyone else at the table, she often felt like she was. And Madison was the one who inevitably had to deal with the fallout from all the trouble the others got into.

"Well, I'm going to check out the casino next door," Gabrielle said. "Anyone coming?"

"Why not?" Amber said. "There's nothing else to do in this god-forsaken city. Yvonne?"

Yvonne stared at the drink before her with furrowed brows. "You two go ahead. I've had enough games for one weekend."

Madison studied her. She seemed a little off. Before Madison could say anything, Yvonne stood up, muttered a goodbye, and left. Gabrielle and Amber soon followed.

"Looks like it's just the two of us," Blair said. "Finally."

Madison murmured in agreement, her mind still on Yvonne. "Did Yvonne seem off to you?"

Blair shrugged. "I don't know, maybe. It's not like she's Little Miss Sunshine usually. How can you even tell?"

"I've known her for long enough to be able to see that something is going on." Madison frowned. "I should go talk to her."

Blair put her hand on Madison's arm. "Madison, it's sweet that you care, but you don't have to mother everyone all the time. Yvonne is a big girl. I'm sure she's fine."

Madison hesitated, then nodded. "You're right. I'll talk to her in the morning."

"Okay, but right now, we're going back to our suite." Blair paused. "You don't actually want to go to bed, do you?"

"Why? What did you have in mind?"

Blair gave her a playful look. "We could open that gift basket Gabrielle gave us."

Suddenly, Madison forgot all about Yvonne. "That's a great idea. After all, it would be rude not to open such a thoughtful gift." She smiled. "But when we open it, we're going to have to test everything out. And I mean *everything*."

Blair planted a tantalizing kiss on Madison's lips. "I'm game if you are."

ABOUT THE AUTHOR

Anna Stone is the bestselling author of the Irresistibly Bound series. Her sizzling romance novels feature strong, complex, passionate women who love women. In every one of her books, you'll find off-the-charts heat and a guaranteed happily ever after.
Anna lives on the sunny east coast of Australia. When she isn't writing, she can usually be found with a coffee in one hand and a book in the other.

Visit annastoneauthor.com for information on her books and to sign up for her newsletter.

facebook.com/AnnaStoneRomance
twitter.com/AnnaStoneAuthor

Printed in Great Britain
by Amazon